AND AN ANGEL CAME TO TOWN

CAROLE A. MANN

Printed in the United States of America

ISBN:	Softcover	979-8-88622-308-8
	Hardback	979-8-88622-310-1
	eBook	979-8-88622-309-5

Republished by: PageTurner Press and Media LLC
Publication Date: 05/24/2022

To order copies of this book, contact:
PageTurner Press and Media
Phone: 1-888-447-9651
info@pageturner.us
www.pageturner.us

AND AN ANGEL CAME TO TOWN

CAROLE A. MANN

CONTENTS

Part One

Part Two

Part Three

Part Four

Part Five

Part Six

Part Seven

Part One

THE FIRST MURDER

It was the "tweening" hour, just before 5AM when daylight begins and gives the stars a rest. Jane was a creature of habit and as she put on her jogging shoes while sitting on the front steps she always chuckled when she heard her grandfather loudly snoring in unison with his dog Frankie right by his side. She loved running the logging trails this early every morning as she actually enjoyed hearing the forest waking up also. She lived with her grandfather in a small house near the edge of town which was only about 15 minutes from the main logging trail. After her daily run which usually took about an hour and a half, she would drive to the local school where she taught English, do a quick change and then start preparing for her day of classes by 7:30 AM. She loved her job, and knew she had a special bond with all her students. As she ran, her mind also raced in its own way. One student always stayed on her mind. His name was Jacob Rosker, a boy who never smiled, was sullen, a loner and seemed to always be filled with anger. She could honestly say he was the only student who she feared in a way. On Monday she had to confront him again concerning his grades. She remembered their first encounter, it was unforgettable for her. As she tried to talk with him and instill the importance of his education, she could actually feel the hate and anger that emanated from him and would always remember his only words to her as he just walked out of class that day, "I don't give a shit, leave me alone or you'll be sorry." He seemed to enjoy the dark anger that clung to him, and never talked with other students. She finally came to the conclusion that Jacob had serious mental problems and was headed down a dark path toward a troubled life. Unfortunately Janie Goldman would soon experience just how mentally ill Jacob Rosker really was.

Jacob hated school and had every intention of quitting when he turned 16 soon. The only time he felt somewhat at ease was when he walked the logging trails, but even then his dark side was still apparent as he found pleasure in using his slingshot to kill and mutilate small animals that he came upon while walking through the endless acres of forest.

The first time he saw her he had kept himself hidden behind a large oak tree, just watching as she jogged by him. It didn't take long for him to memorize her schedule, and he made it a point to watch her routine every morning. Then he contrived a plan that exhilarated him. He liked this new feeling and smiled to himself as he realized he had never felt this level of excitement before.

It took him three days to dig a very deep hole. He made sure it was quite a distance from the trail she always used. He was planning the kill for Saturday morning and had been practicing for hours with his slingshot. He even chose larger stones to use, standing behind the oak tree where he would act on the deed.

That morning he felt almost invisible behind the large tree. The quiet of the forest this early calmed him, then he heard the usual soft pounding of her footsteps as he carefully watched her coming his way. He let her pass about six feet before he silently stepped out from behind the tree, took a deep breath, pulled the slingshot taut, took aim and smiled as he watched the large smooth stone fly and hit its target. There was no noise as the stone hit her skull two inches above her neck. Like a picture in slow motion he watched her fall to the ground with her arms flayed out. A soft thud, and the stillness of her body left few doubts that she had been killed instantly. He walked over and turned Jane's body over. He saw that her eyes were open as if she was staring at the sky. He felt for a pulse just in case, but there was none. It had been a perfect shot, a killing shot and that feeling of excitement he now enjoyed lasted longer this time. He dragged her lifeless body by the ankles to the hole he had dug and pushed her into it. There had been no blood. He had left a shovel near the hole, and as he started to cover her body he also threw the slingshot in the grave with her. When he finished his task, he camouflaged the area with leaves and old branches, also making sure he left no footprints. He then took a large container of ground black pepper and sprinkled it all around the site, even walking backwards quite a ways making sure there would be no trace of him and the pepper would distant any tracking dogs, which he knew would be part of the search efforts. As he walked back through the woods he spotted a shiny object. It was a small gold locket on a chain, that had been broken. He put it in his pocket because he decided he wanted to keep this prize then quickly headed back toward his house though the dense part of the forest. He climbed through his bedroom window which he had left open, smiling to himself as he crawled back under the covers. It was a little past 6:30 AM, perfect timing, since his father always woke the boys up by 7AM. He even had planned a perfect alibi then closed his eyes and replayed his first kill over and over in his mind, with a smile on his face.

Old man Sydney woke up at his usual time when his dog Frankie, a mini dachshund, started to whine and jump around telling him he needed to go out. Sydney started the coffee, grabbed his morning paper, fed Frankie and waited for Jane to come home before he started breakfast. It was Saturday and they had made plans to visit a small craft fair that afternoon. Patience was not one of the old man's attributes as he kept looking at the clock. At noontime, he made himself a sandwich and was getting grumpy. By 2 PM he was annoyed. By 4 PM he was a bit concerned, it wasn't like Jane to not call if she had made other plans to be gone most of the day. By 7 PM he was now anxious and started pacing the floor. When his Grandfather clock chimed 10 PM, he decided to call the Sheriff's office. The answering machine was on but he left a lengthy message. He took the dog for a quick final outside time and when he was walking back into the house the phone was ringing. It was Sheriff Lambert and as she listened to him she knew he was starting to panic. She told him he should come by her office first thing in the morning to file a missing person's report, but he didn't want to hear it. He was just about screaming at her into the phone, saying over and over that something was terribly wrong, and that his Janie would never do this. Her car was still in the garage. He told her he had even called the small clinic but there had been no reports of anyone coming in to be seen for any injuries. He had also called a couple of her teacher friends, they had not heard from her either. The Sheriff told him she would cruise around the town and ask a few people if they had seen Jane. That seemed to calm him down a bit, but she knew it was going to be a long night for Sydney.

By early the next morning everyone in town knew about the disappearance of Jane Golden. The Sheriff had called the State Police who came to town within the hour. Search parties were organized and missing person flyers were being distributed and placed all over town. Search dogs were brought in, even Willy Grey Wolf leashed his dog Molly, a highly trained German Short Haired Pointer, and teams began searching the logging trails and many other parts of the forest. After almost five days of searching, old man Sydney sat on his sofa holding Frankie close and finally cried. Deep in his heart he knew there was no hope.

All the students organized a vigil the fifth night. Jane Golden had been one of the most loved teachers at their school and as candles were lit many tears could be seen. No one had second thoughts that Jacob did not attend the vigil. He just remained in his bedroom, holding the gold locket that had Jane's name engraved on it and smiling. Later that evening when Eli returned from the school, he was certain he had heard strange laughter coming from Jacob's room. Little did he know that one day he would hear that same dark sound again and recognize the why and how of it.

TOWN OF ALTON

Alton was much like hundreds of other small towns. Cottage like homes and various businesses lined the main street. People knew each other and that seemed to draw them closer at times of need.

Some of the first shops that had been established in Alton were Carl's Butcher Shop, The Clip and Snip Barbershop, Ben's hardware store, The What Not Curiosity Shop and Norton's Tavern. Gerry's Diner seemed to be the hub in the town, and was open from 6AM – 7PM with the best food served ever. The Sheriff's office and small jail was also situated on Main St., run by the first woman Sheriff for the past several years. There wasn't much crime in the town. The occasional brawl outside Norton's Tavern, a few speeding tickets and reports of stolen items were just about the only crimes she had ever had to deal with. The Sheriff loved her job and knew everyone by name in the town.

At the end of Main St. was Arel's Gas N Go. It was the only gas station in town and also had a small convenience store. Eileen Arel and her son Dave ran the business. Dave was an excellent mechanic and was always busy, but whenever he did have some free time, Eileen would find him out back in one of the old garages working on his motorcycle, a vintage Harley Davidson Fatboy that he and Willy found at an auction. He now had it running like new and even repainted it a glossy cranberry color. He did grumble a bit though when his mother bought him a matching helmet, and made him promise to always to wear it. He knew better than to try and argue with her, so the helmet became one with the Harley.

The town prospered and the main reason was Bill Rosker Sr. He owned the large sawmill and logging company, and over a hundred acres of pine, maple and oak trees. As his business grew so did the town, drawing families with the promise of steady employment. He ran his business with a logical mind, but also had the task of raising his two sons. His wife had died several years before of breast cancer, but he was determined to raise his boys as he had been raised, with a firm way followed by a love only a father could give. His sons had been born in Alton and would be raised there. He truly hoped they would take over the business after he passed on.

Bill Rosker Jr. was well liked by all the townspeople and also in school. He was an excellent student and participated on the basketball, soccer and baseball teams. He also showed an interest in his father's business. On weekends and during summer vacations he became proficient in every aspect of the business, from taking trees down to milling them for planks and mouldings that were sold all over the state. The employee's trusted him like they did his father. Bill Jr. had a way of being able to train even the newest of workers. After he graduated, there was little doubt that he would continue on at the mill for his career choice.

Bill's brother Jacob was the complete opposite of his older brother. He hated school and dropped out at the age of 16. Bill Jr. knew Jacob was such a disappointment to his father, but always made excuses for him. Jacob knew he better find some kind of job so he worked at the diner, but that only lasted a week.

Rumors flew around the small town about Jacob. He had a slight limp because he had been born with a hip dysplasia, and had an attitude as nasty as a rattlesnake. He would frequent Norton's Tavern but started so many fights he was thrown out and banned from the establishment. He then began a menial job at the sawmill. No one trusted him and all the employees stood clear of Jacob when he walked the main floor of the mill.

One warm day as Bill Sr. walked one of the logging trails he had a massive heart attack and died. The townspeople, employees and his family were devastated, but Bill Sr. was a logical man and had kept all his affairs in order for quite some time. He did this to make sure Bill Jr. inherited the entire business.

VIRGINIA AND MAZER

Mazer and her sister Virginia had been raised by their grandparents. Their grandmother was Cherokee and ran the small farm with an iron fist and a sense of humor. Their grandfather, also Cherokee, was a quiet man with quiet ways and was also blessed by his love of nature. Mazer and her sister Virginia grew up on the small farm learning all the ways of the Cherokee, but Mazer, being much younger than her sister chose her place also as a child of nature. She knew her true name was Amanda and loved to hear the story her grandfather told why she was called Mazer. While a baby, the grandfather would rock her and saw such beauty in the infant. As she grew, her hair was black as an ebony stone, and her eyes were as green as new grown Irish moss. Her grandfather would smile and say to his wife, she will be an amazing woman, hence came her nickname Mazer. She could run as swiftly as the deer in the forest. She learned the ways of the woodlands and was always bringing home orphaned forest creatures. She had a gift of healing and would smile as she brought the healed animals back to their homes in the woods.

Her sister Virginia was ten years older than her and was also a beauty in her own way. Auburn hair, big brown eyes and a motherly air in her nature. She loved her younger sister dearly but would rarely speak of their parents and the accident that had claimed both their lives soon after Mazer was born.

Bill Jr. always attended the town functions and he had a special reason for this. He was infatuated with Virginia and had fallen deeply in love with her. She also realized she had secretly withheld her feelings from him not knowing how he felt about her. After dating for several months he finally found the courage to propose to her, which she happily accepted. Mazer thought of Bill Jr. and Virginia as a "fairy tale" couple, always holding hands and seeing such love in their eyes. He promised to treat her as the queen he thought she was. The logging company prospered immensely. He bought the newest of equipment and built the business into his own small empire. He built Virginia the grandest home in Alton. It sat on a hill overlooking all the buildings, the forest and logging roads. He also made a promise to Virginia that for every tree cut down a seedling would be planted in areas that would someday be full with growth again. He was a good man, and always treated his employees with respect. He was known to help those in need especially whenever Virginia spoke of a family that was struggling.

No one exactly knew when Arthur had first had shown up in Alton. He always wore a camouflage jacket, black hat and army boots, which seemed well worn. He went around to many of the small businesses but never asked for a handout. Somedays he could been seen sweeping in front of the small shops. One day Gerry had hired him to fix the picket fence around the diner. When the job was completed Gerry came out to check the fence. Arthur had done a great job, in fact it looked quite professional. She smiled and asked him in so she could give him a proper meal and pay him his days wages. She was puzzled when he hesitated, but everyone in town knew you never refused Gerry. She took his arm and escorted him inside the diner. It was about 2:30 in the afternoon, and she insisted he sit in a comfortable booth. He asked to use the men's room to wash his hands and when he returned to the booth a look of shock was on his face. A full course meal was waiting for him. He had tears in his eyes, but then said his version of Grace before enjoying the meal. Mike the cook came from behind his kitchen and sat across from him. He put his hand out, introduced himself, and Arthur did likewise. Arthur felt an immediate sense of trust from Mike. "I guess you have a lot of questions?":Arthur said. Before Mike could answer Arthur told him his story:

He had done three tours of duty in Viet Nam, then traveled around since he had no family that he knew of. He had thought that it had been a useless war and Mike agreed. Being African American, a Viet Nam Vet with no roots and poor was not exactly what companies looked for on a resume. When traveling around he had spent the last few years doing odd jobs, and most of the people who hired him had been kind to him. He spoke with a slight southern accent and told Mike he had been raised in the foster care system in Georgia. He said his favorite memories were when a nice family took him in, raised him right and even graduated from high school. He beamed with pride as Mike sat and listened. Then there was an awkward silence so Mike finally spoke up. "Where in Georgia is your family?" asked Mike. Arthur just sat and ate then looked straight into Mikes' eyes as he said, "They're both dead, there was a riot in the streets that day and they were both shot and killed while walking back from the grocery store. Mike, can I tell you something?" Mike was stunned but nodded. "I truly think that our country is so full of hate and racism it will never heal from all the woes it has had to endure." Mike nodded again but then had a "brainstorm", which according to Gerry didn't happen that much. He asked Arthur if he'd be interested in a steady job. Not here at the diner but at Bill Roskers sawmill. He knew the old small bungalow was still stranding and it would be perfect for the old Vet. Arthur finished his meal with a slice of warm apple pie and a cup of coffee, smiled and told Mike "that would be pretty fine by me."

Now all Mike had to do was convince Bill that he needed a janitor and security man full time. As Mike walked back behind his kitchen area Gerry came up to him and asked what he was up to. He took her aside and told her his plans. She smiled, gave him a kiss and said, "You're a good man Mike, but that's why I married you," and walked away. This was Wednesday and the meat pies were still warm.

Mike had it all planned out. He knew Bill and Virginia brought the boys to dinner every Wednesday evening and would have Gerry talk to Bill right away. Everyone that came to the diner that night noticed a smile on Mike's face. As soon as the Roskers walked into the diner Gerry grabbed Bills arm and pulled him aside. She told him the entire story. He smiled and said it was a done deal. He asked Gerry if she or Mike could bring Arthur by the mill after three days. Gerry agreed, told Mike then went to Virginia's booth and told her the latest news.

Bill was always a man of his word. The next two days the renovation of the small bungalow near the mill was now completed with a new roof, new windows, and an updated kitchen and bathroom. A woodstove was donated that could heat the three room bungalow all winter. On the fourth day three cars pulled up and many women from the town piled out an took over, Virginia being the leader. The small bed was made and new curtains went up. The twins from the What Not Curiosity Shop had come upon an embroidered wall hanging that said, "Home Sweet Home." They had found the perfect place to hang it right above the door.

The next day Mike brought Arthur down to the mill as promised. Bill had immediately taken to Arthur. Bill smiled and said, "Well Arthur, you are now our new janitor and would also like you to handle the job of security at the mill. It's not much, just walk the grounds around 11PM so you can keep an eye on the mill. Would you do that for me?" Arthur was still in pretty good shape for his age of 71 and after listening to Bill he seemed to stand straighter as he replied, "I'll be the best damn employee you ever had." This started everyone laughing. Bill and some of the employees walked him to the bungalow then Bill handed him the keys. He smiled and told Arthur this is your new home from now on.

Jacob had also been there. He constantly had an obscene smirk on his face and wished he had been successful the many times he had tried to run Arthur out of town. He felt little compassion for the homeless and also thought he was superior to most of the employees. Jacob hardly cared about anything or anyone. He was a slovenly person and he seemed to have a dark aura always around him and a constant sneer on his face. He .mumbled over and over and actually had an odor about him that many acknowledged when he made an appearance in the mills main shop. He was condescending and rude and frequently swore at the workers. Bill Jr. knew this and had tried talking to his brother, but it always ended in a verbal tirade from Jacob. He had a soft spot because Jacob was his brother. So many times he just walked away feeling disheartened and wondered why his brother had grown up so full of hate and jealously. Sometimes Jacob would just disappear for three to four days, but always returned reeking of whiskey, acting meaner than ever.

CARL-THE BUTCHER, THE BAKER AND THE CANDLE MAKER

Carl B. Swenson was the town butcher. He had learned his trade from his uncle and eventually bought the business when his uncle retired and moved to Florida. He was a very tall man of Slavic heritage, but had never married so had put his heart and soul into his meat business The town still did not have any fancy super markets so his store did a thriving business. He was a quiet man but not because he wasn't friendly. He had a distinct stutter and a mild form of Tourette Syndrome. It seemed like he was always apologizing for the sudden verbal outbreaks when he became stressed with orders backing up, or if the meat slicer didn't work properly.

Passersby would hear the tirade of words, "SHIT, CRAP, SHIT." Then the banging of utensils and more stuttering. The majority of the townspeople just accepted this behavior, especially the two Nuns who taught at the smaller school. Sister Madeline and Sister Theresa always made their weekly run on Thursdays to order a variety of sliced meats and his special thick cut pork cutlets. After paying for their order and thanking him, Sister Madeline always remembered to tell him how he was in their daily prayers. He would just blush and stutter thank you.

His shop was immaculate and he also began baking. The smell of fresh breads, scones and a variety of cupcakes made daily helped pass his time. Since he never married (although there were rumors of a special friendship with Sheriff Lambert), he also found time to enhance his craft at making scented candles. The twins featured his candles at their store, the What Not Curiosity Shop.

THE WHAT NOT CURIOSITY SHOP

Two sisters owned the local gift shop. They also happened to be identical twins, so identical that more than once people would suggest they wear name tags. Two young women who could finish each other's sentences, dressed alike and knew where everything in the shop was placed. All the townspeople knew that no matter what you were looking for, it could be found at this shop.

One part sold clothing, gently used. The right part of the establishment carried everything from pots, pans, plates and all other dinner ware, vintage Knick Knacks, handed down mementos, art pieces and even old photos. In the back of the store was a large glass encased cabinet which held their true treasures - a wide variety of antique jewelry.

Every month the girls would travel to area towns to browse and buy from weekend flea markets and any yard sales they came upon. They always came back with boxes of treasures for their store. The shop had acquired its own idiosyncrasies over the years. The two sisters of course never took notice of this. They just accepted it like the dust that always accumulated on the oddities they sold. They lived in the small apartment above the store, along with their menagerie of various cats and dogs.

THE SISTERS ALL GROWN UP

When their grandmother passed away it was a sad time for the family and also for the town. Mazer then took on the duties of the small farm. She also became more and more aware of her grandfather's failing health. He no longer walked the paths of the great forest with Mazer. He just sat out on the back porch smoking his pipe and mumbling to himself. Mazer knew it was just a matter of time. Their grandfather was slowly dying of a broken heart.

On a typical day at the small farm she saw Virginia drive up. She was so excited she could hardly contain herself. Then she told Mazer the news, she was pregnant. Mazer smiled, gave her a big hug and whispered in her ear, " it's a boy." Sure enough, eight months later Eli was born, a strapping eight pound eight ounce baby boy and on that early eve the grandfather was found in the barn, leaning on a bale of hay with a smile on his face because he too had found solace for his soul. A birth and a funeral. How could anyone control emotions for both. The neighbors helped as much as possible. Mazer was relieved when the last of them left the farm. She was alone now, except for the garden and the animals, and the solitude consoled her, giving her strength and a strong sense of determination that she knew she needed.

As time passed, routine and all their lives held firm. New shops continued to emerge on Main St., and the town continued to grow.

Mazer had finished her schooling a year earlier, but no matter how hard and often Virginia demanded she move to the big house, Mazer stood her ground. She would tell her sister, "I belong here." The farm had been left to her and she was determined to keep it. She enjoyed her solitude, loved her gardening and was becoming quite proficient with her cooking and baking. There was a small detached garage and in it was the pride and joy of her grandfathers. It was a 1966 powder blue Studebaker Cruiser with all the chrome on it polished to perfection. She loved that vintage car. Dave from Arel's Gas N Go taught her to drive it well. He also changed the tires on it and raised the wheel base so she could drive through the acres of logging trails without damaging the under carriage. She had him even install a third type of headlight above the rear view mirror on the outside, with a small handle that could be turned from the inside, giving an extra bit of illumination while driving in the woods. Eileen Arel, Dave's mom and owner of the Gas N Go would just shake her head whenever Mazer told her that the car had a Third Eye. She loved Mazer and had enjoyed watching her grow to be such a beautiful woman.

Eli was growing like a weed and when he turned ten Virginia learned she was pregnant once more. Mazer just smiled, looking forward to becoming the spoiling aunt again, and also knew another boy was on the way. Months later on Mazers birthday, Alex came into the world. He seemed to be quietly looking around, showing off his red hair and light blue eyes. As the next two years passed, Bill Jr. and Virginia would take the boys to town every Wednesday.

They enjoyed their weekly trips to Gerry's Diner, especially on Wednesday when the special was French meat pie. The pies were handmade and baked by one of the old townspeople, Jeanne Boise. If you didn't put your order in or came by for a late supper the pies would be sold out. Even Mazer always had one put aside for her to take home. She a looked forward to the meat pie supper with Bill Jr., Virginia and the boys. Mazer had always been gifted with a strong sense of intuition. This one Wednesday she couldn't help but notice that Virginia seemed worried and distracted. While Bill Jr. was making the rounds at the diner, chatting with Mike the cook, Gerry and so many others he knew well, Virginia was near tears and confided in Mazer that Jacob was stealing from the company.

At first Bill Jr. refused to believe it. Virginia had even sat him down in the kitchen of the Great house to discuss this with him. Bill Jr. knew she was right but didn't have the heart to dismiss Jacob and end his employment. Virginia was relentless in this subject. Little did they know Jacob was lurking at the bottom of the stairs listening intently to both of them. Jacob spit on the floor and smiled an evil grin. He then decided from the darkest part of his heart that many changes would soon be coming. He knew he would have to be careful and clever as he started planning the horrific accident.

That Friday the accountant, Harrison, arrived at the Mill at his usual time. He walked up to the office where Bill Jr. was sitting at his desk and was on the telephone with one of his customers. He sat as he listened to what Bill Jr. was telling John, one of his largest customers. "That can't be right John, I haven't raised the prices for six months. Listen, just pay the regular price on the invoice and I'll get this squared away on my end, ok? No problem, we'll talk this week." He slammed the phone down and looked at Harrison. "Do you believe thus?" just shaking his head. Harrison looked straight at Bill Jr. and said "Yes I do." "What do you mean ?" Bill Jr. said. " Every week I have Jacob go around to pick up the checks for the invoices then deposit them at the bank. How hard can that be ?" Harrison just looked at him, produced several printed out sheets from his briefcase and put them on the desk in front of him. "Look at these" he said, "There have been a great number of withdrawals the past few weeks and some are quite large." Bill Jr. looked over the print outs and his mouth fell open. The accountant looked at him and said, "I hate to tell you this but Jacob has been embezzling from the company and I just showed you the proof." Bill Jr. was furious as he pushed the ON button for the intercom and loudly said he needed Jacob in the office immediately. Harrison left just shaking his head saying good luck with this and walked down the stairs out to his car. Jacob saw him drive away and headed to the big office upstairs And then all hell broke loose.

A huge argument started in the upstairs office. Even the workers on the ground floor were concerned about what was happening. The screaming and shouting quickly turned into a brutal brawl between the two brothers. Bill Jr. towered over his brother Jacob, who again had been drinking and was demanding that he should be given more of a share of the profits. This infuriated Bill Jr., then Jacob took the first swing at his brother, but he was ready for it as he punched Jacob right in the jaw. Jacob went down hard. He knew he was no match for his brother. As he slowly got up he braced himself on the large metal desk, grabbed the lamp nearest to him and flung it at his brother, grazing his forehead and scalp. Blood started streaming down Bill Jr.'s face and that was when he picked up his brother by the shoulders and threw him up against the glass window. All the workers stared, some even stopped the massive saws and lathes. The huge work area became suddenly quiet except for the loud screaming and the sounds of smashing glass. The employees started to whisper to each other as Bill Jr. dragged his brother down the steel stairway and actually threw him out of the building. The last words heard were from Bill Jr. shouting to Jacob that he leave immediately and he never wanted to see him again.

Jacob then began spewing obscenities, but limped away while continuing to throw stones and pieces of re-bar at the building. Blood dripped from his mouth due to a lost tooth which occurred during the brawl.

Bill Jr. walked back to the ground floor of the work area, grabbed a clean rag and started to wipe the blood flowing from the scalp wound. At that moment he noticed the silence, turned and with his hands on his hips, yelled at the stunned workers. "What are you looking at? Get back to work." Bill Jr. let out a sigh as he climbed up the stairway to his office, noticing the workers quickly starting the saws and loading more logs that were to be milled. They turned to look again as the heavy steel door opened and watched as Virginia ran up the stairs two steps at a time while carrying little Alex. All of them knew their jobs but kept glancing up at the office upstairs. Virginia was crying, and tried to calm Bill Jr. down while she hurried for the first aid kit so she could clean the wound. "You have to get sutures, there is too much blood." He could hear Virginia but still was in a state of anger. "I don't need stitches" he said, finally calming down so little Alex would stop crying. "We're going to the clinic and I don't want any arguments" Virginia said. That's when Bill Jr. knew he would not win this debate. Virginia packed up Alex while she held a bandage to Bill Jr.'s head. About twenty minutes later he was being examined by Doctor Horton who said, "Yep, you're going to need about ten sutures." Bill Jr. glanced at Virginia's smug look, smiled and said, "I hate when you're always right."

Two hours later they returned to the Great house. The shop was closed and locked up. Bill finally laid down, feeling calmer now and went to sleep. Virginia made it a point to check all the windows and the back door to make sure they were securely locked. She tucked Alex in for the night and also peeked in Eli's room to see if he was asleep, which calmed her down. She realized she was still pacing the floor in the kitchen, thinking about Jacob. She was not looking forward to the next morning, but finally shut all the lights off and walked upstairs to their bedroom to try to sleep also.

There are rarely few secrets in a small town. Sure enough, the next day just about everyone knew what had happened. Even Sheriff Lambert drove her cruiser to the Great house just to make sure everything was fairly back to normal.

Bill Jr. had a headache and was laying on the sofa enjoying the quiet Saturday.

The shop was closed for the day. Three of the workers had come in just to clear the broken glass and check the office for any other dangerous debris. Bill Jr. was thinking about the entire incident and trying not to get upset again. Little Alex was on the floor playing with his toy trucks and Eli went to a friends for the afternoon.

There was a knock at the front door as the first of many concerned townspeople came to visit and offer any help. She opened the door while wiping her hands on a dish towel. Carl the butcher walked into the living room. He was carrying a package that he handed to Virginia and shyly said, "Its Bill Jr's favorite" and smiled. He had driven his white van up the dusty road to the Rosker residence. Everyone called it the Great house. In the package was some special cuts of beef for them and also a lavender candle. Virginia gave him a big hug and little Alex bounded over to Carl for one of his famous shoulder rides. Carl absolutely adored the young one and would always bring him a special surprise when he returned from his weekly trips to the wholesale meat market three towns over.

He wanted to hear about the entire incident from Bill Jr. but knew few words were needed. He had heard the whole story from Sheriff Lambert, especially about the odd disappearance of Jacob. No one had seen him leave or knew where he was now hiding out.

He played with Alex and stuttered some truck sounds that always made Alex laugh and beg for more. This had made Carl's day, but soon he said his goodbyes to all and headed back to the butcher shop. He had an uneasy feeling and vowed to visit more often. Virginia had told him he was always welcome and that brought a smile to his face, but that uneasy feeling about Jacob still lurked deep in his heart.

The next visitors were the twins from the Curiosity shop. They brought an apple pie, some special incense, and a crystal of rose color that they guaranteed would bring positive energy to the Great house.

Bill Jr. was now up and around, feeling better and looking at the fresh pie the girls had brought. He was slicing a large piece, even though

Virginia gave him that look, the one only concerned wives could give. She said her good byes and thanks to the girls, but kept glancing out her kitchen window at Mazer. Mazer was outback shaking her head as she vigorously pulled most of the weeds from the small garden Virginia had planted. Mazer loved being an Aunt, and spoiled both boys endlessly. She was truly looking forward to Sunday night. She had talked Virginia into letting both boys sleep over at the farm. She had big plans for this special event, some quality Auntie time. Virginia had agreed because Monday was going to be a somewhat hectic day at the Mill. Bill Jr. had said he wanted to have an employee meeting explaining what had happened between he and his brother. He wanted to reassure his workers that there would be no changes at the Mill. It would be business as usual especially since they were behind almost two days and had three large orders to complete.

Virginia packed the boys clothes up and gave her usual instructions to Eli when he came home. She gave him a hug, but frowned when she thought she smelled perfume on him. She had her suspicions about Eli having a girlfriend, who she thought was Jenn Pinkton. She had talked to Bill Jr. about it, but he just laughed and said, "Virginia, boys will be boys, even if he is only twelve." She gave him that look again while she watched Mazer and the boys drive down the road in her car, that stupid Studebaker and just shook her head. Little did she know at that moment that so many changes were about to happen. She closed the main door and suddenly realized how quiet the house was, almost too quiet, but was looking forward to a good night's sleep after the hectic day.

Part Two

Cecilia's Purpose
Jacob's Revenge
The Great Fire

CECILIA'S PURPOSE

Mazer always knew she had a special spark, that shine that gave her the gift of intuition. She believed in Angels and had even met her own guardian angel. She had dreamt of her many times and tried to heed her messages. While walking through the forest one day when she was very young, she experienced an approaching great white light which took her breath away. She knelt because she knew it was her Angel. She told Mazer her name was Cecelia Blue Fern and one day she would be called upon to carry out a great task as would her Angel. Mazer was in awe, especially with Cecelia's wings. The Angel was so beautiful and as she put her hands on Mazers head, visions were shown to her, but Mazer was just a child knowing only childish ways. The Angel knew this also but Mazer's faith was true and she was a blessed one. She had been chosen for a special purpose many years from now and only then she would realize just why she had been assigned a special task.

There was a loud buzzing near her and she woke with a start. She looked around and yawned and couldn't believe she had fallen asleep in the forest. She also remembered she had been dreaming, that same dream that she continued to have since a child. She stood up and brushed herself off, then saw a large bumble bee and understood the loud buzzing sound, but that was just a dream, wasn't it? I'm not a child anymore as she headed back to the farm. She smiled as she saw Olsen the cat trying his best to stalk a dragon fly. He's getting so fat, she wondered how he could even jump on the sofa which was his favorite place to nap. She thought about her dream again and wondered why she could remember such a dream that had bewildered her since a child. She picked Olsen up and walked into her garden and sat under her favorite tree, a Magnolia, and felt a chill, still confused about the dream. She felt silly and shook it off as she watched Olsen now trying to catch a butterfly. The dream was so real and its memory clung to her as it always did, even as a child. The visions were getting stronger and for some reason she felt a great responsibility was coming to her, the same one that had been shown to her when she was young..

JACOB'S REVENGE

Arthur had decided to make his security rounds a little earlier that evening. For the past two hours he had cleaned and refilled all the seed and humming bird feeders. He had a special place in his heart for birds. Every morning he would sit on the old stump outside of his small home and have his coffee while watching the variety of birds that would just about cover every feeder. He was always amazed with the humming birds, and also became familiar with the distinctive calls and songs of the other birds. He even practiced calling back to them which began to arouse their curiosity. That always brought a smile to his face.

He put his jacket on and walked to the Mill, checked his watch and saw it was about 10 PM. When he put his key in the lock of the back door he was surprised to find the door was already unlocked. He walked around the main floor turning corners and checking that every machine had been shut down properly. All of a sudden he felt someone behind him. He turned but didn't have time to press the red alarm button which was only a few feet away. He felt the massive blow to his head and as he hit the floor his last thoughts were, "whose going to feed my birds?"

About II PM Virginia woke up to the smell of smoke. She shook Bill Jr. awake and they both dressed quickly. An argument ensued because Bill Jr. was heading to the Mill and Virginia was right behind him. He started shouting at her, "No Virginia, it might not be safe!" She looked him straight in the eyes and said, "All the more reason to go with you." Again he knew he couldn't convince her to stay at the house. He just stomped out the door, but she was right behind him. It only took a half hour to see that the entire Mill would soon be engulfed in flames. Small explosions were going off every ten minutes. He knew the trucks and machines were gone, but he thought he might save something as he and Virginia ran in the back way. Right away they couldn't breathe and saw the stairway to the upper office was smoldering. All the large windows had blown out and much of the smaller machinery and tools had even melted somewhat where the logs being stored downstairs were now burning. He stood in shock thinking my life, my business is destroyed. Little did they realize two large propane tanks were behind one of the main conveyor belts. That was the final explosion bringing the remaining roof and large rafters down upon them. Bill Jr. and Virginia were buried in debris and the end of the Mill took them with it.

THE GREAT FIRE

Eileen Arel had been tallying the receipts for the day when she heard the first siren. She looked at the Esso clock above the counter and saw it was 12:21AM. She went out the front door to look for David and the smell of smoke hit her full force. When she heard the second siren she felt a feeling of fear come over her. She went back inside, grabbed her keys and ran over to her Land Rover. With her tires spinning out the driveway she headed quickly to Mazer's farm.

Mazer was already up. She checked the boys, and saw Alex was still fast asleep. Eli was sitting on the side of his bed. He had a look of confusion on his face, but began putting his boots on and followed Olsen the cat into the kitchen where Mazer was opening the door. The ash and smoke was swirling around with every gust of wind. Large flames could be seen quite a distance away, but Mazer knew the fire was just starting to gain strength. She shivered knowing that because of the dry season they had and the acres of large pines, oaks and maple trees not yet cut would be fueling the fire.

Almost all at once Eileen, Sheriff Lambert and Carl were at her door. She told Eli to run down to Jeanne's house to ask her to come watch Alex.

Sheriff Lambert had sent Dave to the next town which was about fifty miles away to arrange for help from their Fire Department. Alton only had two fire trucks and one pump truck, which was getting on in years.

They all walked to the small hill behind Mazer's farm. Eli was back with Jeanne Boise who patiently sat with Alex as he still slept. Jeanne could hear the sirens and her nerves were working overtime as she bit her nails.

The twins came and walked up the hill where the others stood watching the flames grow higher. Buttercup and Hannah were growing more and more tense so Eli went quickly to the barn and gave them extra hay to help calm them down.

More sirens could be heard but they were still far off. Eileen was beginning to worry about her son, knowing how Dave flew on that motorcycle of his. All of a sudden the radio in the Sheriffs cruiser crackled. She talked and listened a while as the others waited to hear any news. There were so many questions and no one knew what had happened. Mazer had a distinct bad feeling in her stomach as did Carl. They both looked at each other and waited for Sheriff Lambert to finish her call.

The Sheriff put the radio down and looked at all of them. She told Eileen that Dave was fine. He was driving along with other fire trucks. Sheriff Lambert took a deep breath, looked at Mazer and said the Mill is burning. At that moment there was a huge blast and they could see flames shooting in to the air that was almost twenty feet high. The wind was blowing easterly and pushed the fire with such force. There were more blasts and the flames seemed to be sweeping over much of the forest.

Mazer was holding Eli back. He wanted to go to the Great house to get his mom and dad, but even Carl and the others made him realize he had to stay at the small farm.

Many forest animals were fleeing the fire. Deer, moose, bear and smaller woodland creatures could be heard almost like a stampede toward the small gorge at the end of the logging trails. The river was low but there was still water running. Hopefully it would be their safe haven. Carl thought it was a good idea to hose down around the small farm, so they all untangled two of the long hoses and started to spray the house and barn. Every time they heard trees crashing and felt the earth tremble, all they could do was pray.

Suddenly they saw several truck lights heading toward them and recognized them all. On the outskirts of town there were three farms. The first one was owned by Tom Choate, he raised pigs. The second was Nick Bernstein, he grew corn, soy and also had a few acres of alfalfa and timothy grasses, which he baled every year and sold. The third farm was owned by Willy Grey Wolf. He had dairy cows, milk goats, three horses and many chickens, ducks and geese. His true love was his dogs, which were German Short Haired Pointers. Every year his Molly had six to ten pups, healthy, pure bred and sold all over the state.

Truck doors slammed and all the men that came with them were covered in ash and soot, many coughing and wiping their eyes. Rosie had actually walked all the way to Mazer's farm and even though she was known as the cranky old lady next to the diner, she began barking orders to everyone about getting water and wet towels for the men.

Mazer had had enough. She walked to the garage and opened the front bay door. She wanted to drive down to the Great house to make Virginia and Bill Jr. come back to her small farm. She knew their house was far enough away from the huge Mill, plus it was on a hill, but she had to know they were safe. The smoke was getting thicker and fiery ashes were blowing everywhere. As she opened her driver's side door Eli was right next to her. "No Eli" she said, but he was as stubborn as his dad. He started to argue with her. "I'm not a kid any more Auntie Mazer, I'm going. I have to know that my parents are okay and you can't stop me." He had tears in his eyes but she knew he would stand his ground on this. She fumbled with her keys not knowing how to handle this. She was happy to see Gerry from the diner drive up. She had brought all kinds of sandwiches, hot coffee and a fresh batch of cupcakes Carl had delivered that evening. She knew how worried and stressed Mazer was. She gave her a big hug and told her that everyone in town was up and about. Mike the cook and many of the employees had headed down toward the Mill. She stopped there not wanting to give Mazer and the others the news that she had been given. Mazer stared at her and kept saying, "Tell me, tell me Gerry, I need to know." Gerry looked down at the ground, shifting her feet and fighting the tears back as she held Mazer by the shoulders and quietly told her that the Mill is gone. Most of the machinery and trucks were beyond saving and from what she was told acres of forest was still burning. The Wildfire Rescue Teams were battling one of the biggest blazes in years, but it seemed it was a losing battle. No one said a word. Mazer and Eli went back into the house, not knowing what to expect next.

It took over three days for the Forestry Division to work the over one hundred acres that had burned. They divided into teams to make sure any smoldering fallen trees and stacked logs that had not been brought to the Mill yet were not burning. The entire forest looked like an apocalyptic scene. The fire had spread east and south after the Mill's final explosion. The flames had been seen for miles. The smoke and ash still permeated the air around the town, and many of the towns people were hosing the ash and soot from their homes and vehicles. The massive destruction had many in a state of shock.

Mazer was pacing back and forth. The authorities would not let her near the Mill or the Great house. Even Olsen the cat was finding solitude in his favorite places that he hid in.

The Chief Fire Inspector had been at the Mill for over two days now, investigating just what may have started this massive fire. He had promised he would have some information late that afternoon and would come by to give Mazer a preliminary report.

Sheriff Lambert had called her that morning to let her know she would accompany the Fire Inspector. The Inspector's name was Jack Statern, and he also had known Bill Jr. and Virginia personally. As he walked through the rubble and charred remains of the Mill, he had been the first to find the bodies There were three, all unrecognizable, but made sure that all three of the remains had been taken to the state coroners for a full examination. He was puzzled, why three? He had interviewed all the employees, hearing about the explosive argument between the brothers. The more he learned and the more he investigated he was convinced that Bill Jr.'s brother, Jacob, was not one of the fire victims. This finally came to light when several of the older employees confided that Arthur, the old custodian and part time security man Bill Jr. had hired years ago, had not been seen or heard from in over three days.

Around 4PM that afternoon Willy Grey Wolf, Carl, Eileen and even Reverend Weinberg arrived at Mazer's farm. Jeanne Boise had taken little Alex to her house, but Eli refused to go. He told his aunt he was old enough to hear the truth and would not budge. This exasperated Mazer even more. She had so many decisions coming. She knew she would take custody of her nephews, but would also have to meet with the lawyer and accountant concerning the business. Then there would be funeral arrangements, and as she thought this it finally hit her and hit her hard. Her life would never be the same nor for the boys either. Gerry from the diner had come by early again, and also other neighbors with food or to offer any assistance.

Mazer finally sought some privacy out near her garden. Olsen jumped on her lap and she held him and sobbed for almost an hour. She felt someone standing behind her and saw Willy Grey Wolf. He placed his hands on her shoulders, wishing he could take some of this pain she felt away, or at least lessen it. He had watched Mazer grow to be a responsible and beautiful woman, inside and out. He knew she had a question and did not think it odd when she asked it. "Uncle Willy" she asked. He just looked her straight in the eyes and nodded a bit. "Do you think the two hundred and fifty year old maple, you know the one that sits right at the end of the ravine burned?" Uncle Willy just stared off in the distance for a few moments and then shook his head. "I just don't know Mazer. How about I promise you this, when things calm down a bit, you and I will take the Studebaker and ride out there?" Mazer slowly shook her head then heard Eli who had been standing in the doorway say, "I'm going too, and don't even try and talk me out of it." Willy smiled, crossed his arms and just shook his head. He looked at Eli and said, "There's a great big story about that tree son, one that has been passed from generation to generation in this town. You sure your up to hearing it ?" Eli was a strong young man, already so tall like his dad and still growing. His sense of seriousness impressed his Aunt Mazer and Willy Grey Wolf as he said, "At this time in my life I am ready to hear anything, and think I deserve the truth spoken to me as any man would." Mazer looked at Willy and said, "I think you should tell it ." He again nodded, sat on a nearby stool and started the story: "Eli, that great maple is about two hundred and fifty years old. Some of its roots alone are as large as the limbs. It is scarred in strange ways when someone first sees it, but then when you look more closely you realize it has many initials and messages from the carvings of so many people passed. It still grows straight and true, it's leaves turning a bright red in the Autumn. Over the years it has been home to so many birds, squirrels, chipmunks and owls and all have left their mark in a way. Every year two Peregrine falcons come to nest in one of its highest boughs. Some of the carvings were made long before even my time, but I do know your grandparents, my brothers, and even some of the original townspeople have left their mark. It's almost like a tradition. Mazer and your moms names are there, also your dads and his brother. The Cherokee call it, the Tree of Stories and people still make the long trail hike out to that old tree. The story about it was even in the town paper once. I even remember the three Lancaster boys who all had carved their names and birth dates before leaving for the war in Vietnam. Almost a year later all three brothers were killed in an ambush near Laos. Their parents moved away after that, but not before they themselves drove out and carved their own initials and messages in the tree. Someday it will be time for you and your brother to do a carving of your own, and the tradition will continue on. What also makes the great tree so special is that it grows on a bank right next to the ravine. Right below it the river runs and it just hangs on as though the Great White Spirit has balanced it perfectly. If you ask me, I don't think any fire would be powerful enough to take down that tree. It has been blessed by the beautiful energy of so many people, and I do believe it will continue to do so."

There was a stillness then, and the quiet was noticed by not just Mazer, Willy and Eli, but others that had silently gathered around to hear the story again. Some had their heads down, praying in their own way. Others had tears from memories of their own about the Tree of Stories.

Some of the listeners were returning to the house while others started preparing the super meal, and you could hear the noise of plates and silverware along with quiet chatter. Mazer rose from her chair and hugged Eli. She knew there was another official story he would hear soon and she worried about how that would affect him. She heard the rumbling noise of an old motorcycle pull into the driveway. It was Dave, Eileen's son. As he took his helmet off and settled the bike, he seemed far away in his thoughts. His mom went out to greet him and he was talking quietly to her making sure no one was around. Mazer couldn't hear Eileen and what she was saying to Dave, but then he blurted out, "Oh Ma, I can handle it, trust me." They both came into the house and Dave greeted everyone, and said, "I'm starving, what's to eat?" That seemed to lighten the mood for a while. As they were all eating and enjoying the vast assortment of food, that mood changed suddenly as all of them saw Sheriffs Lambert's cruiser and two official State SUV's pull up. They all heard car doors slamming and the doorbell ring. Mazer got up from the table to let them in. She felt a bit light headed but knew she had to be strong.

The Chief Fire Inspector, Sheriff Lambert and Dr. Horton stood in the doorway. Gerry from the diner came up to them and asked if they had eaten, saying there's plenty of food still on the table. They declined but thanked her anyway and just asked for coffee. All three were escorted to the small living room and their coffee was served. Olsen the cat seemed a bit miffed because he was shooed away from his favorite spot on the sofa. Olsen seemed to take pleasure in his own cat routine, like putting on a show. He stretched, rolled over and gave a big yawn. Then the twenty pound cat slowly pranced away. When he smelled food, his eyes (which one was yellow and the other green) lit up and he sauntered over to the table. His manners improved and he sat patiently for someone to notice. It worked because Gerry had already made a special plate for him, and set it down near his water bowl. He looked at her and it made her smile, then started enjoying his blue plate special. Gerry knew how much that cat meant to Mazer and just shook her head and thought he's the most spoiled cat she's ever seen, but she knew Mazer would be lost without him. She quietly stepped back into the living room and prepared herself for the news coming, and she knew it would not be good news.

Jack Statern, the Fire Inspector coughed and cleared his throat. He began shuffling papers around which he had taken from a manila folder he had brought with him. He looked at Mazer and then started his verbal report. You could hear a pin drop before he spoke.

"Mazer, I've spent over two days going over the big Mill and all the other buildings. I even walked through the entire Great house. I started at 6AM every morning until 8PM every night. Sheriff Lambert was nice enough to let us bunk out at her place, so we both had lots of time to talk this through. Now, I believe it was arson, and as you already know your sister Virginia and her husband Bill Jr. were killed in the Mill fire. He waited a moment, hearing some people gasp and even saw others close their eyes and shake their heads. Willy Grey Wolf spoke and said, "I heard there were three bodies found, who was the third victim? "Jack looked at Willy and stated professionally, "We believe it was Arthur, the part time security guard that Bill had hired a while back. Between the gasoline used to start the fire and all the propane tanks, it didn't take long for the massive fire to spread.

The Forestry Division has estimated that about seventy five acres were nearly destroyed, also all the other machinery and trucks left out on some of the logging roads. The business is a complete loss, and I'll put that in my report. I know Bill Jr's. insurance company are going to have a lot of questions. I already spoke with his lawyer, Charlie Baker. He also owns the small bank where Bill Jr. did his business." He looked at Mazer and said, "I'm pretty sure they all will be contacting you soon." There was a deep quiet in the room Just the antique clock above the fireplace could be heard ticking away. No one knew what to say, so many chose to be speechless out of respect for Mazer. Carl the butcher got up and walked into the kitchen. He was so angry, which set off a tirade of swearing and everyone could hear his fists pounding the kitchen counter "Shit, Crap, Shit, damn him, damn him to hell." Then they heard him sobbing while still letting any foul language flow from his lips. The Tourette's Syndrome was taking over. Dave quickly walked into the kitchen to calm him down, and console him in any way possible.

Now it was Mazer's turn. She felt such anger. She became flushed and turned to Jack, "What about Jacob? Where is he ? Hasn't anybody seen him? We all know Jacob did this."

Sheriff Lambert took over now trying to keep everyone calm as she told her side. "No one has seen or heard anything about Jacob, even all his drinking buddies from Norton's Tavern. I checked the basement apartment at the Great house, seems like a lot of his personal belongings are gone, like he is. I put an official warrant out for him and all the other police officials have been notified, they are looking for him also. I just don't know where to start. No one even knew where he had come from when he came to Bill Jr's. and Virginia's. He didn't drive, did not have a license or bank account. I think Bill Jr. paid him cash because there aren't even any employee records for him. I just don't know. I will tell you this, I will not stop searching and investigating I promise you." Things seemed to be calmer in the kitchen with David and Carl. Jack once again looked around at everyone. It seemed he had tears in his eyes as he spoke again. "This had been a terrible tragedy, one none of us will probably fully understand or even get over. I know how all you people take care of each other in so many ways. So now is the time you must stick together and keep your eyes and ears tuned. I really feel Jacob is still out there somewhere biding his time."

That was when Eli stood up. He looked around but addressed his question to Sheriff Lambert. "Sheriff?" She looked at him and felt such sadness for this boy. "Yes Eli?" she replied. "Do you think Uncle Jacob will try to return and claim any rights to my dad's business? Could he do that?" Sheriff Lambert sighed and explained that any proof that could have been used to arrest Jacob had been destroyed in the fire and any finger prints, DNA, any physical proof is now nonexistent.

Once again, many people started to throw endless questions toward her. Mazer hushed everyone then looked at Eli. "My beautiful nephew, I promise from the bottom of my heart that that will never happen. You know what kind of man your uncle was, a liar, a coward and a drunk. For him to be able to do what he did to his own family is unspeakable, and because of that I cannot ever even think of him being able to come back and face all of us."

The people in the room all nodded in agreement, and that was when Eli broke down into tears and sobbed. "My dad, my mom, I still can't believe this. I feel like an orphan." Eileen Arel had been next to Eli when she put her arms around him. He turned toward her embrace and just broke into sobs again.

Mazer looked over to Doc Horton and he knew she was asking for his help. He moved over to where Eileen and Eli were, whispered to Eileen and took one of Eli's arms. "Come on boy, let's see if we can get you to rest a bit." Eli went right along to the spare room in the back. He was so tired and not because he had had so little sleep in the past two days, but was just so tired of thinking about things. Eli was able to sleep for three hours. Mazer and Eli were sitting on the sofa later. Evening darkness had set in, but every now and then a small gust of wind would stir up more ash and soot from the fire, just enough to bring back more painful memories of the fire. Most of the townspeople had said their goodbyes and Mazer knew many of them would stop by again soon to offer any help. The twins from the What Not Curiosity Shop had also come by. They were in the kitchen doing dishes, putting leftovers away and tidying up in any way just to keep busy. Carl and Dave had returned to the living room and were quietly talking with Willy Grey Wolf. Sheriff Lambert eyed Willy, and knew what was on his mind and how he was plotting with Carl and Dave for revenge. She slowly walked over to the three men, shifting her belt and holster almost as a sign that she was in charge, that she was the law. She looked at all three of them and spoke softly, but with a direct tone she knew would make them understand. "Boys, I hope you're not even thinking what I am feeling here?" "And what might that be?" Willy replied. "This is a small town and I do not want to hear rumblings about any means of revenge." She continued to look sternly at them and saw that Carl would not even look her in the eye. "I'm just saying, I've always believed there is a fine line between justice and revenge, and I have every intention of getting to the bottom of this terrible incident. Do we understand each other?" she said sharply. All three looked at her and nodded. "Well" she said again, "I hope this is the only and the last time I have to talk about this to the three of you, ok? Again they all nodded. She walked away but she could still feel how they were plotting in some way. For her it was just going to be another thing to keep her eyes on, especially Willy Grey Wolf. He had a temper and several times she had broken up brawls he had been involved in. He was a righteous and stubborn man. He seemed to have calmed down a bit over the past few years, but she would still keep her eyes on him. Like her old grandmother had always told her, "You can't change a penny." She thought about that and Willy was a prime example.

Jack and Doc Horton had left, so had the twins and Gerry. Eileen and Dave were outside now going to head back to Arel's Gas N Go. Carl passed her and touched her shoulder lightly, said good night and was headed back to the butcher shop to check it and lock up.

Mazer and Eli were still sitting on the sofa along with Olsen the cat. Before leaving, Sheriff Lambert gave them both a kiss and a hug and said her goodbye's. She told them she would be back tomorrow.

Mazer was so tired. She knew that tomorrow she would have to start the funeral arrangements and since Jack Statern said she could go to the Great house now, she wanted to gather up the boys clothes and anything else they wanted. She told Eli she was going to bed early, but had given him permission to go to one his friend's house. She knew all his friends would be there and felt he needed that comradery at this time. He promised to be home by 10PM and she knew he would. She gave him a big hug and kiss and he was out the door. She slowly walked to her bedroom with Olsen the cat right behind her. She fell asleep easily and once again dreamt of the Angel. Cecilia Blue Fern had slowly flown over the small town. She could see and feel the negative energy that was growing and was saddened about the chaos and confusion that surrounded Alton. She sensed so many good people there, but also realized that many did not know what to do about the conflict being expressed in so many different ways. She felt anger, sadness, fear and distress. The people were outwardly distraught. There was shouting and words of rage and it hurt her ears. Cecilia slowly unfurled her gigantic wings. As a darkness surrounded her she thought storm clouds only obscure the universe of light, but never diminish it, and she watched and waited for the outcome of Alton.

Part Three

PRESENT DAY- TEN YEARS LATER

When Olsen jumped on her she woke with a start. She noticed it was light out, rubbed her eyes with the palms of her hands and looked at the cat. He had a look on his face and she knew that look. It was a, 'Hey, I'm hungry and you'd better feed me now' look. "Big old lazy cat," she said. She stroked his thick coat, remembering how she found him half-drowned as a kitten. She nursed him with love and luck, and sure enough he was now a near 20 pound gray striped tom cat. She loved this cat so much, and he knew it. Wherever Mazer was, Olsen was always right behind her, even in the barn and especially in the garden. She couldn't imagine being without him. Even the way he looked at her with those eyes, one green and one yellow, she spoiled him to no end and to her he deserved it. She got up and walked to the kitchen. She couldn't believe she had slept that long. She also was a bit bewildered by the strange dreams of so many memories. She filled Olsen's Kibble bowl and gave him fresh water. She put the tea kettle on, but this time she would have a large cup of coffee. She was going to need that boost of caffeine. Tomorrow was a big day, not only was it the anniversary of the big fire, but Eli was leaving. He had joined the Marines and was leaving for his second tour of duty in Afghanistan. She hoped he would be back at the farm later saying his good byes to Mazer and Alex. She also knew where he had spent the night. She smiled to herself, looked to Olsen and said "Ah, the passion of the young." Olsen continued eating, the only passion for him right now was filling his stomach.

ELI AND PINKY

Eli was softly snoring as she lovingly stroked his shoulder then cuddled up to him as close as possible. She had known as early as second grade that Eli was the one. She loved him so much and she knew that that love was returned tenfold.

His duffle bag was packed and placed near the door. His uniform was washed, crispy pressed and hung on the coat rack near the door also.

Two evenings before he had told Mazer and Alex that he was he was leaving for his second tour of duty. Mazer looked confused and Alex barely touched his food. Eli spoke with an air of certainty as he told them he still needed more for his life, and felt the Marines would provide that now and after.

Mazer gave him a big Auntie hug. She was so proud of him. He had grown to be a fine young man, six foot three inches and slim like his dad. He had thick dark auburn hair and also his dad's smile and mannerisms. Sometimes from afar Mazer thought she was seeing Bill Jr. Both Bill Jr. and Mazers sister Virginia, had perished in the Mill fire ten years ago.

His second tour of duty had been his decision, and it was set in stone. He was leaving again the next morning. His close friend Roger Elison was deploying with him also on this second tour of duty. He was picking him up early the next morning so they could take the bus from the nearest station, which was about thirty five miles away.

Eli woke and stretched and held Pinky in his arms. He noticed she was just staring at him, but then kissed her and smiled "Well" he said, "Tomorrow is the big day." He saw tears in her eyes and he kissed her again. "Don't be sad, I'll be back in six months and then we'll have enough money saved for a big wedding. Remember that is our plan." She wiped her eyes and smiled. She also reminded him that there was a farewell party at Gerry's Diner tonight. She had picked out the perfect dress, a light pink chiffon that was sleeveless. Everything she owned was pink, or some version of that color. Her parents had passed away several years ago and she had inherited the house. Ever since she had been a small child she had been mesmerized by the color pink. She had had the house painted light pink and a darker pink for the trim and shutters for an accent color. Surrounding the house was a white picket fence with different colors of pink roses, peonies and many more varieties of pink flowers. She tended to them with loving care and was the envy of her neighbors. Inside the house it was immaculate. Her bedroom had been decorated with several versions of mauve. Her sofa was a dark rose color and even many of her accessories had a pinkish hue. Pale pink sheer curtains hung from the big window in the living room, and next to her antique piano her grandmother had left her, was a cage for her pet Cockatiel, who was also pink with a touch of white feathers. The bird talked and mimicked constantly. His name was Charlie short for the color of chartreuse. She had a spare bedroom and small den. In the den was her sewing machine. On the shelves were stacks of patterns and also yards of material, of course mostly pink. Her kitchen was an off white color, but her pans, plates and cups and kitchen wall hangings all had some version of pink. She loved her bathroom. It was larger than most, her window dressings, towels and shower curtain were again pink, just different hues. Pinky prided herself with her little house. She took in mending, because sewing had always come natural to her. She truly enjoyed the challenge of making dresses and was fastidious about her sewing.

She had been a waitress at Gerry's Diner for about five years now. She had grown to be a beautiful young woman, five foot six inches tall, slim with shoulder length blonde hair and dark blue eyes. Not only was she Gerry's best employee, but through the years Gerry had treated her like the daughter she never had.

Everyone who came to the diner were always treated with respect as she smiled at all of them. Her cheeks always blushed a rosy pink when the old farmers came in and flirted with her. They all knew she was Eli's girl and so many commented what a perfect couple they made. Tonight would be special. All the townspeople would be attending the farewell event.

As she was making breakfast for Eli, she remembered what had happened after the Mill fire. Since the Mill had been the main source for employment in the town, so many families had to make the difficult decision concerning their future. At first, business at some of the shops almost came to a halt. Many of the residents had little choice but to pack up and move, hoping to find employment in some of the other nearby towns. Even Rosie, her cranky neighbor across the street had said Alton was going to be almost like a ghost town soon. Pinky tried not to believe it, but after eight years she realized it could soon be true. Entire families left, some trying to sell their property or even just trying to rent them out. The video store had closed, also the tailor from the Knit and Sew. The larger of the schools stood empty and boarded up, as did one of the churches. The hardware store was still open, but just about hanging on. Even Norton's Tavern had seen a decline in customers, so the owner changed the hours it was open for business. The small theatre and computer store were also now closed.

Sister Madeline and Sister Theresa had started teaching the children left in the town, plus Jeanne Boise volunteered her time to teach some of the older children. Even the remaining farmers were getting nervous. With no rain and fewer prospects of supply and demand, they were often heard grumbling at the diner. Tom Choate was still planting, but had made a deal with Eileen Arel. She had a small lot a little ways from the Gas N Go, so she let him open a farm stand there. Nick Bernstein, one of the other farmers, continued his crops and hay bailing, but transported most of it about sixty miles away to the large farmers co-op there.

Rumors spread about the drought The sky had an ominous appearance with the strangest clouds. They looked rippled and elongated, the color of light and dark gray, plus they never seemed to move. It looked the same every day. Mazer had heard so many of the old wives tales implying that the town was being cursed. She had even begged Reverend Weinberg to be a little more upbeat in his sermons, but even then he only held Mass twice a month now.

Arnie at the barber shop, The Clip & Snip was still open. As was Carl the butcher and the What Not Curiosity Shop, which helped with some foot traffic on Main St. Mazer noticed a difference in her garden, but at least she had two deep wells so everything was watered enough. Willy Grey Wolf would come by twice a week to fill his large containers on one of his trucks. He made sure all his animals had sufficient water.

As Pinky thought all about this after her shower she said a little prayer. Her new dress fit perfectly and she was brushing her hair as Eli came out of the bathroom. He was dressed in his uniform and looked as handsome as ever. He gave her a hug and asked what time they had to get to the diner? Pinkie replied about 6:30PM and they still had plenty of time. Eli noticed she seemed a bit distracted and nervous. He went and put his arms around her and said, "Babe, everything is going to work out, you'll see." She gave him a big smile and decided to keep her secret a while longer.

MAZER KEEPS A PROMISE

Mazer had washed and changed. She was waiting for Alex to get home. He had started a little lawn mowing business but was usually on time. She paced a little, looking and seeing that it was almost 5:30PM. She finally heard him skid to a fast stop near the driveway. Two years ago Willy Grey Wolf came upon a great bargain on an almost new bicycle for him. They had painted it red and Dave at the Gas N Go checked all the tires, the gears and gave it a good once over. She had a big argument with him about wearing a helmet. He was always flying around on that bike way too fast. He told her he loved to feel the wind, she told him you'll love to feel my old wooden spoon on your back side not as much. That ended the argument and she had found a good helmet for him at the What Not Curiosity Shop.

She could also hear his dog, Cooper. They were inseparable. She remembered about three years after the Mill fire, Carl had appeared at the door with a puppy. He was a purebred German Shorthaired Pointer. It was love at first sight for Alex and that puppy. He named the pup, Cooper. Alex now had a best friend, and through the years with the help of proper training from Uncle Willy, Mazer couldn't think of a better gift. The dog was loving, obedient and protective of Alex every minute of the day.

Last year, on one cold winter day, Alex had fallen through the ice while exploring a small pond. Cooper grabbed him by the collar of his jacket and pulled him out to safety. Both were fine, but it was the talk of town for weeks.

Alex ran in the house with Cooper at his side. He looked at Mazer and said, " I know, I know I'm late." She pointed to the bathroom and said, " Shower now!" She had already laid his clothes out for him, and put Cooper's food out. The dog knew they were leaving him in the house for a while tonight, and gave Olsen that look. The two of them got along fine but Olsen was the boss. Alex came out of the bedroom dressed, but still drying his hair. "What about Buttercup and Hannah?" Alex asked. Mazer had told him she had already cleaned their stall, fed and watered them. She finished towel drying his hair, checked his ears and fingernails as he rolled his eyes. "Aunt Mazer, I'm not a little kid you know, I'm not a baby." She smiled as she replied, "You'll always be my baby." He shook his head and went back to the bathroom to brush his teeth.

Mazer went to the kitchen, wiping the counter down one last time and she happened to look in the direction of the Great house. She took a step back, she could swear she had just seen a light in one of the top windows. She didn't move and kept watching, then the light went out. She could feel the hair prickle on her arms and had a strange feeling in her chest. Her logical side thought it might just be a reflection, but there had been no sun at all, especially since those strange clouds encompassed the town. Alex startled her as he came up behind her. With her hand to her throat she took a deep breath. "Oh! I thought I saw a strange bird." She hated to lie but found little reason to worry Alex in any way. She turned around and looked at Alex, " How handsome you look ." He blushed as he usually did then got all excited when he realized that they were taking the Studebaker tonight. "Please" he begged "please?" "One condition" Mazer said, "Cooper stays in the house, okay?" Cooper thought Alex had given in too quickly, and finally strolled over to his bed and plopped himself down, but not with his happy dog face on.

Mazer jiggled the keys and gave them to Alex. He ran out to pull up the garage door and to start the Studebaker up. He loved this car. He couldn't wait to be old enough to drive. Many afternoons Mazer, Alex and Cooper would pile into the car and explore all the logging trails. They knew them all by heart and she had even let him drive the Studebaker a couple of times, but slowly. His Aunt Mazer had kept her promise also. One day a few years ago, she drove Eli and Alex out to the old Maple tree. She had been so grateful when Willy Grey Wolf had come by to tell her it had been untouched by the fire. When they arrived at the tree, Eli and Alex were more than amazed. Here was this great tree, over two hundred and fifty years old. The Tree of Stories stood before them almost clinging to the forest floor that overlooked a gorge about ten feet away. The ridge there was straight down and the river flowed peacefully as it had for many years. Mazer took out her knife that she always carried, handed it to Eli and said, " It's your turn to add your story and your brothers." Eli took the knife and carefully carved his and Alex's initials into the soft bark of the tree. Before he finished, Alex wanted to carve Coopers name. They laughed, but Alex did a good job. Eli stood silent as he found his parents initials, and was in awe as his fingertips traced so many more. Some he had no idea who they were. He could sense a whisper in the wind and realized that the Tree of Stories stood for a reason and Mazer agreed. That had been one of their greatest days, one they would come to cherish in the years ahead.

She heard the horn honk a couple of times. She hurriedly grabbed her purse and fanciest shawl, gave some last minute instructions to Cooper and Olsen the cat. Cooper just whined a bit, but Olsen could care less. He took up half of the sofa space as he laid on his back with his legs in the air. Just a spoiled big old lazy cat. She had to have a talk with him tomorrow because she had found some mouse droppings in the barn, and that had always been his job. She slammed the door and headed to the garage. She saw Alex at the wheel of the Studebaker and smiled. "Slide over boy, let's get going.." She loved this car. It was a 1966 Studebaker Cruiser. It even had the famous Hawk logo on the wheel covers, the grill and on the engine. The ID emblems were on the front fenders. It had been her grandfathers and he reveled in teaching her all about the car and the history of the beautiful auto. Under the hood, it had the larger 230 cubic inch, 140HP six cylinder engine that had been an option only with an automatic transmission. It had a stylish grill, revised side trim and luxurious interior. The car had been kept in meticulous shape. It also had a refresher ventilation system. The Studebaker had a larger exhaust system and Alex loved the 'varoom' sound as they headed toward Gerry's Diner. "Someday this will be my car, right Aunt Mazer?" She smiled and nodded. Alex had a grin from ear to ear. "And just think, we get to take it out twice, tomorrow is Wednesday and the diner will be having French meat pie night." She didn't say anything because she had a few things on her mind. She had made a mental note to speak with Sheriff Lambert about the light she saw in the Great house. She finally replied back to Alex, "I haven't forgotten about tomorrow night, but then you have to promise me old Lola here (she had named the car years ago) will get a good washing and waxing." "I know I know," said Alex, "Because that helps to keep her in good shape, right?" She chuckled, " That's right sweetie, and we want it to last for a long time. Before you know it, it'll be yours." She thought again of all the times she had taken the boy cruising through the forest on the logging trails. Most of the deadfalls after the fire had been cleared, and new saplings were popping up everywhere. When they arrived at the diner they were amazed at how crowded it was. Mazer parked on the other side next to Rosie's small cottage. They both could hear laughter and music coming from the diner. Alex was so excited as he pulled Mazer across the street.

THE PARTY

As they entered the diner Mazer and Alex were astonished at how many people had arrived to celebrate the sendoff for Eli. All the regulars were there of course, even Sister Madeline and Sister Teresa. A large banquet table had been set up and there was so much food available. Alex said, "See ya later, and rushed to the food table. Mazer scanned the room and finally saw Eli and Pinky, and of course a large crowd had them surrounded. She made her way over giving hellos and hugs to everyone she met along the way. She was almost there when Eileen and Gerry grabbed her arm. They both seemed to be teary eyed. Eileen gave her a big hug and said, "Our boys are all grown up, where did the time go?" Gerry leaned over and whispered in her ear, "We really should have a serious talk soon." Mazer smiled and once again started making her way through the crowd. She noticed Sheriff Lambert all dressed up and having an intense private conservation with Carl the butcher. He was excitedly going on about the new state of the art meat slicer he had just purchased. Mazer smiled a bit when all she saw was stars in Sheriff Lambert's eyes. She finally had careened through the crowd of well-wishers and gave Eli one of her famous Auntie Mazer hugs. She had tears in her eyes and such pride in her heart. She saw how beautiful Pinky looked and also gave her a big kiss on the cheek. "You both look so happy which makes me so happy." She started some small talk, "What time are you leaving? Do you have enough money?" And said three times, " I am going to miss you so much ." Alex wiggled his way through the crowd and jumped into his big brothers arms. Eli held onto him and reminded him that he would now be the man of the house until he returned. "I know, I know Eli" he said. "I have it all planned out."

All of a sudden everyone began singing, "For he's a jolly good fellow" as Eileen and Gerry carried a large cake (pink and white of course) and set it on a smaller table next to Eli and Pinky. The energy in the room was overwhelming, so many smiles but also so many tears. Even Mike the cook had come out from behind the kitchen area and was seen wiping his eyes. Mazer was beaming with pride, and not just for Eli. It had been such a long time since she had seen so many of the townspeople so exuberant. She was standing near Gerry and chatting when Jeanne Boise came up to her. Jeanne gave Eli and Pinky a hug and laughed when Eli mentioned how much he was going to miss her meat pies. She smiled, but then turned toward Mazer and quietly asked if she had seen Rosie at all. Mazer thought for a second, "Now that you mention it, no I haven't. Maybe she just decided to stay home, after all she is eighty years old." She could sense that Jeanne looked concerned and asked why. "Well" Jeanne said, " I've called her two to three times today and there's no answer. Also, no one seemed to have seen her out at all today. That is so unusual, I knocked on her door, and I could hear the television on, you know how she loves her game shows." Mazer herself felt a twinge of concern. "Maybe you should mention this to Sheriff Lambert, just to be on the safe side." Jeanne shrugged and said, "She was probably just sleeping. I really don't want to make a big deal out of it. I'll try calling again later." Jeanne started talking to Pinky. She eyed the cake and put two slices on her plate. She thought she'd save one for Rosie.

The festivities continued, people laughing with a lot of back slapping and Marine stories being told to Eli. Mazer finally caught sight of Alex and nabbed him as he quickly walked by, "There you are little man." She noticed he had cake frosting on his shirt and both of his pockets were bulging a bit. "What have you got there Alex?" He blinked and whispered, "I snuck some treats for Cooper and even a bit of chicken for

Olsen." Mazer grinned and gave him a hug. She told him not to wander off too far because they would be leaving in a while. He said, "Ok," and dashed off again.

She started looking around for Carl and Sheriff Lambert. Now she too felt a bit concerned about Rosie. She just wanted to give Sheriff Lambert a heads up. She knew it wouldn't hurt and would also ease Jeanne's mind a bit. She eyed them by the punch bowl and was able to slide through the crowd to where they were standing. Greetings were exchanged amongst them and comments about the great turnout. Mazer leaned over to Sheriff Lambert and whispered she'd like to talk with her for a moment. She repeated what Jeanne had confided in her and the information peaked Sheriff Lambert's interest. She promised to check in on Rosie first thing in the morning. Mazer felt better now, and was satisfied that Sheriff Lambert would check out Rosie's place. She scanned the room, saw Alex was with Eli and Pinky and started over to them. She knew the difficult moment was coming for her since this would be the last time she would see Eli in quite a while. She stood before the couple and gave hugs and kisses again. She promised Eli she would take good care of Pinky, but also knew that Gerry would take that task to hand before anyone else. Pinky was quiet, she seemed a bit disconnected from the entire party. Mazer had noticed it previously but also realized Pinky had so much on her mind. Pinky stood still, knowing Mazer was in her scan mode. She looked around Gerry's Diner and realized how much she loved the place. There were three waitresses employed there and Pinky was the head waitress. When she had first applied for the job years ago, she just knew the position was for her, because the waitresses uniforms were pink.

The diner itself was a vintage quality and about two thousand square feet. It had about sixteen booths with dark green table tops and chrome trim. Each booth still had a small juke box attachment where the customers could flip through a number of titles and play their favorite songs. The counter wrapped around about one half of the diner, again having a dark green counter top and lots of chrome like the booths which was polished daily. The floor was a lighter green tile and that too was washed and waxed every evening. At one end of the diner was a small dance floor and a large juke box. It opened at 6AM and as soon as you entered, the smells of fresh brewed coffee, warm muffins, scones and donuts filled the air of the diner. The menu board was changed daily and the diner was known as a town icon. From area farmers, truckers and townspeople, business was always brisk. The kitchen area was a sparkling stainless steel, and all day people were used to hearing the bell ringing and Mike the cook shouting, "order up." The diner was Gerry's pride and joy and her life. She spent about sixteen hours a day there but loved every minute of it. Fresh meats came daily from Carl's butcher shop, along with his bakery goods. Eggs came from Willy Grey Wolf's farm. Tom Choate, one of the area farmers, supplied the diner with fresh vegetables and fruit. Of course, Wednesday night, Jeanne Boise's meat pies were the special and always sold-out. Gerry had missed so many of the families that had to leave town after the Mill fire, but made sure one of the off white walls displayed pictures of many of them. She knew they created memories to talk about, especially the large picture of Bill Jr., Virginia and the boys, Eli and Alex, taken many years ago.

As the last of the well-wishers left, she also told Pinky she could take the next day off, but Pinky said no, she would just come to work a little later. Gerry saw Eli standing and looking at his mom and dad's picture, He took Pinky's hand and turned to Gerry and her husband, Mike the cook and said, "Make sure you keep the memories, I love you guys." Then out the door they went.

Mazer and Alex arrived home around 9PM. Cooper of course was right at the door to greet them and followed Alex everywhere while sniffing his pants pockets. He knew treats when he smelled them. After he gave Cooper a small treat that he had smuggled home, he put the rest in the refrigerator. He was brushing his teeth when Mazer was getting his pajamas out. He was a bit annoyed as he watched Aunt Mazer and said to her, "You know, I'm going to be thirteen soon, I can get my own pajamas. I'm not a little kid anymore." He saw the look his Aunt gave to him, and felt a little embarrassed. "Sorry if I came off as being a bit huffy." He had never remembered any time that his Aunt had been angry with him. They had a wonderful close knit way between them and he never wanted that to change. He quickly put his pajamas on in the bathroom and then jumped into bed. Aunt Mazer stood and waited with her arms crossed. Now he felt bad and hoped he had not hurt her feelings. Cooper jumped on the bed as she came over to Alex. She looked him straight in the eyes, kissed him on the forehead, shut the light off and wished him sweet dreams. Cooper just looked at him, and Alex just hugged his dog and said, "I think I better apologize first thing in the morning, what do you think Cooper?" The dog gave a soft whine and then they both headed for dreamland.

Mazer smiled to herself, changed into her night dress and gave Olsen a bit of chicken. He meowed while rubbing against both her legs then jumped on the counter purring as loud as a toy train. She grabbed the kettle thinking a cup of tea would be perfect right now. She hadn't realized how tired she was As she reached into the cabinet for her tea bag and cup and saucer, she froze at the kitchen window. There, up on the hill, she saw a definite light coming from the top floor of the Great house. She put on her glasses and watched the light shine from window to window then just disappear again. The sky was still a murky gray so she knew there could be no reflection from the moon, even though it was almost full. Then she thought maybe it was Eli, saying his own good bye to the house. That's just silly she thought. The Great house had been sealed and boarded up long ago. Willy Grey Wolf and a few carpenters he knew had spent three days making sure that no one could enter the Great house. The house was visibly in protected mode. Even Benny, who owned the small hardware store had brought nails and tools needed and also joined the crew. They hadn't boarded up the top windows knowing no one could get up there. But now she wondered. "Damn," she said to herself. She had forgotten to mention the light she had seen the day before to Sheriff Lambert. The Sheriff had told her quite a while ago that she made monthly trips up to the Great house, walked around and checked everything out. It had become a routine and Mazer had thanked her. There had never been any mention about plans for the house, but she had hoped that Eli and Pinky would someday consider taking it over when they started their own family. She definitely would call the Sheriff in the morning. She finished her tea, shut the lights off and went to bed. Olsen was already there taking his side up. She was sound asleep as soon as her head hit the pillow, although she again felt that disturbed feeling which brought on the strangest dreams lately.

ELI LEAVES FOR DUTY

6AM came to quickly for Pinky. She had been up since 5AM that morning to make a good breakfast for Eli. He had his uniform on again and Pinky felt so much love and pride for him. He tried to keep the conversation light because he knew she was on the verge of tears. His good friend Roger Elison would soon be picking him up, but Pinky continued to fuss over him. "I'll write you every day," she said, and send you tins of goodies. I'll even send you pictures." He was hugging her when he heard the horn out front, looked in her eyes and kissed her so hard it took her breath away. "Eli, you promise me you'll come home safe, and always write when you can, now you promise me !" "I will hon, I promise, plus you'll be so busy the time will fly by and before you know it I'll be back, Ok?" The car horn went off again. Now she was crying as Eli grabbed his duffle bag and headed out the door. Roger waved to her as he and Eli drove down Main St. She closed the door and cried for quite a while. Still sniffling, she changed into her pink uniform. As she buttoned it up she thought it felt a little snug. She smiled, grabbed her keys and purse and headed out the door herself, still holding her secret close to her heart.

Part Four

SHERIFF LAMBERT

She was up and about early, made her daily coffee and put on her uniform. She had been the Sheriff in the town for over thirteen years and was a definite creature of habit. Her cruiser was always in tip top shape. She ran her small office efficiently and with an air of professionality. Her hours were usually from 8AM until 7PM, but of course could always be reached by phone while she was home.

It was just about 6AM when she left her house that morning. She was going to meet Carl at the diner for a bit of breakfast before she went to her office. As she backed out her cruiser, she did not hear the phone ring over and over, and the two messages that had been left on her machine. She drove down Main St and often thought how odd it was that many of the small businesses were next to so many of the cottages where people lived. After the mill fire years ago, so many people had left Alton. It seemed to her that as the town grew smaller, the citizens of Alton grew closer. She had convinced herself that was a good thing.

She arrived at the diner, parked in her usual space and walked in. It was busier that morning as she heard many of the customers still talking about the party the night before. She saw Carl at the counter and sat next to him. She knew there were rumors about her and Carl, but smiled to herself thinking, Oh, if only they knew how much they loved each other. Carl looked at her and said with only a slight stutter, "What are you smiling about?" She just shook her head and put her usual order in. She did feel a bit hungry that morning. She stirred her coffee. The food arrived and she watched Carl dig right into his order of bacon and eggs, while even buttering his toast and side order of pancakes. He had a large glass of chocolate milk. He didn't drink coffee because he thought it made him stutter more and as he sipped at it with a straw he asked her what her plans for the day were. "Funny you should ask that sweetie." This was their usual morning banter "I'm going to go check on Rosie, remember Mazer talked to me last night?" He nodded, and she continued, "Then do some paper work I put off that the state requires every month. I'll then take my usual ride through town and also the nearby farms. Sound Good ?" He again nodded. This was the way it was every morning, she talked and he listened. He loved it and he wouldn't have it any other way.

They both finished eating, he paid, she tipped. She had always wished she could give him a good bye kiss but knew it would be the talk of the town for weeks. She touched his shoulder and shifted her belt that held her holster and her gun, a Glock 9MM and walked out the door. She looked at the sky, there was still no sun or rain and watched those strange clouds that never seemed to move.

The twins, Christy and Jody were heading for the diner and they stopped for a few minutes to let the Sheriff know they would be out of town for three days. They were going antique shopping and would appreciate it if she would check the store for them while they were gone. She noticed Christy staring at the clouds also. Jody had her own theory and mumbled that she had never seen such strange clouds all her life. The Sheriff agreed, wished them a safe trip and headed to the cruiser.

She unlocked the office door, picked up the mail on the floor and saw her message machine was flashing. She pushed the button and heard

Mazer's voice, reminding her about Rosie. The Sheriff had planned on heading over to Rosie's in about fifteen minutes or so. She pressed the button for the second message and heard Mazer's voice again. This time Mazer seem distraught and worried, she had seen lights on at the Great house. The Sheriff picked up the phone and called Mazer right back, but there was no answer. Odd but not unusual, Mazer did not have an answering machine, so Sheriff Lambert planned to ride out to Mazer's place after she checked on Rosie. She flipped the sign over on the door that said 'Be Back Later' with her telephone number on it, and quickly walked to the cruiser. She parked on Main St. and waved to Arnie at the barber shop.

When walking up the steps to Rosie's front door, she could hear the television on. She knocked on the door several times, then rang the bell. She knocked louder the second time, then went to one of the front windows. She could see the television on and scanned the room. All of a sudden she stopped. She saw one of the lamps on the floor, and a cup and saucer that had been smashed. She also noted that the bedroom light was on. She tried pushing the door in and even kicked it hard two times. The door didn't budge. She ran next door to the Clip & Snip barber shop. She shouted for Arnie who was sweeping out back. "Arnie, I need to use your phone, it's an emergency!" He ran from out back and said, "Sure, sure right on the counter. What's the matter, what's wrong?" She didn't try to explain, just quickly dialed Carl's number. He answered on the third ring and knew right away something was not right. "Carl, Carl" she was now shouting into the phone. "I need your help, come to Rosie's house and bring a crow bar right away." She hung up and started to think. She ran back to Rosie's and quickly walked around the house. She saw there was no way to get in, even the windows were not close enough to the doors. She heard a truck pull up out front and saw Carl. She could already see his Tourette's syndrome was in full force. He was stuttering non-stop and almost spitting out the words, "Shit. Crap, Shit." She didn't waste any time trying to explain the situation to him, she just pointed to Rosie's front door and said, "I've got to get it open." Carl just looked at her and stammered, "Why didn't you just say that ?" He stomped up the three stairs, lifted his right foot and kicked the door in with such a force splinters of wood went flying everywhere. "Ok ?" he said. She just shook her head, snapped open her holster and started inside. "Don't touch a thing" she reminded him. "I know, I know." She slowly went into the living room, taking mental notes for the report she knew she would have to write up later. Her gut already told her something bad had happened. She took a right into the small kitchen but nothing seemed to be disturbed. She passed the tiny bathroom and noticed some towels all over the floor. Down the short hall to the bedroom, she took a deep breath and walked through the doorway. She just froze. Carl was right behind her. "Oh my God" she said softly. She felt her stomach turn and thought she was going to lose her breakfast. Carl was already running to the small bathroom and she could hear him retching up his breakfast. The smell in the room was overpowering. The Sheriff saw Rosie on the bed and both her wrists were tied to each bed post. Her legs and arms were severely mottled and bluish in color. Her eyes were open but very bloodshot. The Sheriff knew why. She could see a dark thin cord around Rosie's neck, with a piece of paper laying on her chest. It was a note and on it were the words "This town is going to die." Her mouth was open and her tongue was also blue. She knew Rosie had been beaten and strangled to death. Carl came out of the bathroom wiping his mouth, "Sorry" he said. He looked into the bedroom again and thought poor old Rosie. The Sheriff grabbed Carl's arm and as they quickly exited the house, she started talking. "I've got to call Doc Horton, the county coroner and the State Police."

When they were outside she handed Carl a roll of Police tape from the cruiser. He knew what to do because watching police shows on television was his favorite past time. He wrapped the tape around each banister to block the entrance to the front door. He and the Sheriff noticed people gathering out front. She was on the two way radio in the cruiser and the people were starting to ask questions. Jeanne Boise walked up to Carl and said, "What happened, where's Rosie, Oh my

God. I knew something wasn't right, tell me Carl?" she shouted. Sheriff Lambert got out of the cruiser and stood right in front of Jeanne. She knew that Rosie and Jeanne had been good friends for years and felt she deserved to know. She took both of Jeanne's hands and said, "Rosie's dead, she was strangled. My guess is that it happened over a day ago. I just called all the proper authorities. This a crime scene now. I am so sorry Jeanne. I really am." Jeanne felt the tears in her eyes but just turned and started walking to her small truck. It was Wednesday morning and she had a meat pie delivery to make.

Gerry saw Jeanne park her truck in front of the diner, but she just sat there gripping the steering wheel. " Oh boy," Gerry thought, " now what?" She told Mike to get one of the boys to help bring the meat pies in. She walked out to the truck and looked at Jeanne, who told her the horrible news. The order was brought in, then Jeanne pulled out of the parking lot. Gerry just stood for a minute, then walked back into the diner. So many people were staring at her, even Pinky. Gerry sighed and said, "I have some bad news everyone, Old Rosie is dead." Gasps could be heard from all over the diner. Then Gerry finished her statement. "She was strangled, murdered." After those final words she just walked into the back to her small office and shut the door. The news of the terrible incident spread like wild fire. In a small town it doesn't take much for that to happen.

Mazer had never answered her phone. Old Bill Simons, one of the farmers who lived on the outskirts of the town was also the local farrier. He had come by to trim Buttercup and Hannah's hooves. He usually came out about every two months. He looked forward to the visit. Mazer always had a nice lunch for him and they both had the chance to catch up on any town news. Neither one of them knew about Rosie yet.

Alex was off mowing a couple of small lawns. Olsen sat with Mazer as Bill started putting his tools away. She had already put a big box of fresh vegetables and some of her famous lemon squares in the back seat of his truck. That was his payment and he loved it.

As she watched him drive down the road, her and Olsen headed toward the house. She stopped short, looked at Olsen and said, "good job." There was a small mouse lying dead on the first step. She looked at the cat and swore he looked like he was grinning with pride. She disposed of the cats 'bounty' and saw Olsen sitting next to his Kibble bowl. "No way you old cat, you're getting way too fat as it is and moussing is one of your jobs anyway." She heard the phone ring and was happy to hear Pinky on the other end. Pinky was a bit breathless as she told Mazer all the news about Rosie. Mazer was shocked and saddened, and she promised she would stop by the diner soon. She just sat on the sofa, hoping that the Sheriff had received her message about the lights she had seen at the Great house. Between the constant strange gray skies, Eli leaving and now an actual murder in the small town, even she felt a little edgy. She would try to call the Sheriff again later, until then she laid on the sofa with Olsen next to her and feel asleep with ease.

The murder investigation was still in progress, but finally Rosie was laid to rest a week and a half later. The service was short and simple, but all of the townspeople came out of respect. Rosie had one nephew who lived in one of the big cities. No one had even known about him, but he made the trip down for the service. He started cleaning her house out. He sold what he could then loaded up a rental truck, still leaving a few pieces of furniture behind in the house and headed back home.

Things started changing in the small town. People seemed more sullen, plus the constant gray clouds and lack of rain had so many worried. Willy Grey Wolf was at Mazer's one day and told her how many of the farmers were very worried. Some seemed even scared in a way, remembering the draught before the big fire at the Mill. Mazer understood and helped Willy fill his big water tanks from one of her wells. Alex ran over before Willy left and got one of his famous Uncle Willy's bear hugs. They waved good bye as he drove off and Alex said he was hungry as usual. Mazer could see so much of Eli in Alex He was growing taller every day. She often wondered where the time went. As they ate supper Alex was telling her some of the latest news in town.

Alex thought that this was big news and he excitedly talked nonstop for quite a while. He told her there had been two break ins in three days. The hardware store had been one of them. One of the others was the small clinic that Doc Horton ran. He said nothing much had been damaged or taken, but it sure was keeping Sheriff Lambert extra busy. Mazer thought about this and again meant to ask her about the light in the window at the Great house that she had seen several times.

Tomorrow she had a special lunch date in town. Every so often she met with Eileen, Jeanne and Gerry. The four of them would sit at the back booth at the diner. They would eat, laugh at the latest rumors and talk about town events. She always enjoyed their special lunch.

Sure enough, the next day was just as cloudy as the day before. Those light and dark gray rippled, puffy clouds never seemed to move and everyone in the town talked about it all the time. She gave Alex explicit instructions since he was going to stay at the farm. Today was his chore day, but she promised to bring him back a surprise. As she drove off she saw him putting on his work boots while sitting on the front steps and Cooper trying to play 'stick' as he did it. She walked into the diner and saw her three friends already sitting in the back booth. She glanced around for Pinky but saw she was waiting on customers. Eileen slid over as Mazer sat in the booth. Eileen had snuck in a bottle of wine and giggling could be heard as she poured some into four plastic cups. They made a quiet toast, then Gerry said, "I have big news, Pinky is pregnant!" All their mouths dropped. Mazer said, "What, how do you know this?" She was scanning the room looking for Pinky. Gerry leaned forward, "I've had my suspicions for over a couple of months now, and today we should confront her." Eileen downed her wine and smiled because standing at the edge of their booth was Pinky herself. She looked at all of them and said, "Who wants to go first?" All the girls got up and hugged her. Mazer was stunned but happy in her own way. Then the questions started. "How far along are you? How do you feel? Does Eli know? What does the doctor say? Is it a boy or girl, do you know yet? How did this happen?" Pinky blushed when Eileen downed her second cup of wine and said, "I think we all know how it happened." Pinky calmed them all down and started to tell them that no, Eli did not know when he left, but she had written him the day before to give him the news. She was almost seven months pregnant and it was a girl. All the girls at the booth were amazed. Jeanne looked at her. She told her she didn't look seven months pregnant. Pinky had purposely started wearing looser uniforms and she told them that Doc Horton thought the baby was going to be a tiny one. She also said she felt wonderful. Mazer did think she had a special glow about her. Gerry finished her second cup of wine, stood up and said, "Ladies, I have two words" and she shouted "Baby Shower!" Mike the cook looked over, he knew about their special lunches He just laughed and shook his head, rang the bell and also shouted, "Order up."

Pinky went back to work, relieved that she finally told the Big 4, that's what she called them. A special name for special ladies. She had not told them that she had decided on a name for the baby girl yet. She was going to name the baby, Charlotte Pearl. She also had started to redecorate her small den, and of course it was going to be pink. She was so happy and couldn't wait for Eli to return from this special assignment. Her perfect husband to be, her perfect baby and her perfect friends. She had a perfect life. What more could she ask for. Every day she thanked her Angels, and continued to glow as she worked. Mazer and Alex would sit at the kitchen table three nights a week and both wrote letters to Eli. It had become somewhat of a weekly ritual, then Alex would ride his bike to the small Postal Office at the end of town the next day and send them off. Sometimes Mazer baked brownies and lemon squares. She wrapped them well, then rewrapped them again in one of her coffee cans, then wrapped that can again and Alex would send that off also. She called it "Treats for her sweetie." They had received two to three letters in the past seven weeks. She wished there had been more. She would watch Alex come back from the Postal Office with so much disappointment on his face. Many times she had reminded him just how busy Eli was, especially if he was on a patrol. Alex would nod, but he told her he missed his brother so much.

He was still mowing lawns and kept his money in an old jar in his underwear drawer. Mazer had asked him once what he was saving up for, he just replied, "Can't tell, it's a surprise."

When she had told Alex he was going to be a uncle he was so excited, but went "Yuck" when she told him that Doc Horton said it would be a little girl. "As long as the baby is healthy, right?" Mazer said. "Yea, I suppose" Alex replied. He then went out into the front yard to play 'stick' with Cooper. Mazer watched them for a while. That dog could jump so high and grasp anything Alex threw up in the air. She still couldn't believe how devoted Cooper was to Alex.

Mazer glanced at the Great house again. She was convinced that she had seen a light several times now glowing in one of the top windows. Sheriff Lambert had taken a ride out there, but found nothing out of place. She had told Mazer the house was still boarded up nice and tight. Willy Grey Wolf and his friends had been thorough when they secured the Great house after the Mill fire. She told Mazer she had looked for any evidence of cigarette butts, foot prints, candy wrappers or anything that would cause her to think that someone had been there. All she found were prints of deer, coyote and wild turkeys, nothing else. It was unfortunate she hadn't walked another hundred yards from the back yard. She would have found something which might of helped to stop the series of events coming that would change the small town forever. Mazer still kept her eye on the house, especially late in the evenings. She had an ominous feeling and could not dismiss it. She had learned at an early age to always trust her intuition, and this was one time that it seemed so crucial to do so.

OLSEN THE CAT

It was another Wednesday already and the clouds still hung over the town. It made the days seem so dismal. She told Alex to take a quick shower when he came in from finishing his chores. She had promised him they would go to town and have supper at the diner, it was meat pie night. She thought they both needed to get away for a few hours, plus she wanted to check on Pinky.

She fed Olsen and Cooper and checked the back paddock to make sure Buttercup and Hannah had enough fresh hay and clean water.

The routine started when she jiggled her keys. Alex grabbed them and ran out to the garage. She glanced around the room. She left a small light on then she heard the car rumbling and the sound of the horn. Soon they were on their way into town, both hungry for food and great company

They walked into the diner and right away Alex saw Carl sitting at the counter. He jumped on the stool next to him. Mike the cook was leaning on the counter, talking seriously with Carl. Hmm, grown up talk he thought. Mike returned to the kitchen because he knew the diner would be filling up soon. Carl looked pensive and deep in thought. All of a sudden Alex was grabbed from behind and hugged. "Uncle Willy" he shouted, a smile on his face. Willy sat down next to him and said to Carl, "Anything new?" Carl didn't reply right away, but then said, " I guess you haven't heard?" Willy and Alex both just shook their heads no. Carl started telling them as best he could about the What Not Curiosity Shop. Evidently, while the twins were on a buying trip someone had broken into the store. Now Alex could see a deep look of concern on Willy's face. Arnie came in then. He had just closed up the Barber shop, even double locking the front door. He took over telling what had happened, which made Carl sigh with relief. "Isn't it terrible, the girls just got back from their three day trip early that morning. They went into the store and started screaming. I had just opened up and I could hear them, sounded awful." The diner became quiet and many of the customers were trying to listen to Arnie. Arnie continued telling Carl and Willy and of course anyone else who was listening. "Just awful" he said, " There were clothes all over the floor. All the cups, saucers, dishes, even two of the old lamps had been smashed to bits in the front of the shop. The glass case in the back was shattered and a bunch of the vintage jewelry was stolen." All there suppers came. Mike the cook brought them out personally and kept saying, "Just terrible ." He looked at Arnie before walking back to the kitchen and said, " Did you tell them about the note?" "Oh yeah, there was a note left on the counter next to the cash register. A real scary one too, it said, "This town is going to die." No one spoke at the counter. Carl hadn't even touched his meat pie yet. Alex was just pushing his food around his plate then asked them all, "What do you think that means ?" Mazer stepped in and said, "It means there's a bad person in town, but I'm sure Sheriff Lambert will find that person soon." She decided then to mention the lights she had seen in the top windows of the Great house. Willy slammed his fist on the counter, looked at Mazer and said, "Damn it Mazer, why didn't you tell us that when it first happened?" He seemed a bit angry and Carl was just shaking his head. "I called the Sheriff and she checked the house but she couldn't find anything." Dave, from Arel's Gas N Go had been leaning on the counter next to Carl. He looked over to Willy and said, "Maybe we ought to take a drive up there tomorrow and check things out again." "Good idea" Willy said and Carl was also nodding again. "I want to go too" Alex said. " I'll bring Cooper, he can sniff out anything." That's when he heard Aunt Mazer behind him. "Don't even think about it Alex, the men can handle this. You're staying at the farm with me." Alex swallowed a piece of his meat pie then grumbled, "Crap, I can't wait to be a man, you miss all the cool stuff when you're a kid ." They all smiled, then Uncle Willy told him not to worry, he would stop by the farm after checking the Great house and keep them posted. "Ok?" Aunt Mazer said she was going back to her booth with Jeanne. She told him to finish his supper and save room for dessert. They had his favorite, chocolate cream pie and that seemed to brighten Alex up. Around 7:15PM, Mazer made her way to Alex. "Almost time to go little man, finish your milk." Pinky came over to say good bye and Alex couldn't believe it. Her stomach was popping out. So that's what pregnant meant. He didn't want to stare, but Pinky took his hand and placed it on her stomach. His eyes opened wide when he felt the movement. Pinky was beaming and said, "That's your little niece." He felt a bit embarrassed but gave her a kiss on the cheek and said good bye. Aunt Mazer had been watching and thought maybe it was that time for the "birds and bees" talk. She would leave that to Uncle Willy and thought it should be soon.

Everyone was still talking about the break in at the What Not Curiosity Shop. Before you knew it everyone in town would know. A few said they were going there in the morning to help clean up. Their little town, with such good people, Mazer thought.

Gerry came over holding a small paper bag. She had an extra piece of chocolate cream pie for Alex. He was elated and gave her a giant hug and said thank you. On the way out Aunt Mazer said to Gerry, "Time for one of our lunches soon" and winked. "Darn right" Gerry said. "Eileen will be back later and we'll set it up. We can talk about the baby shower okay?" Maser agreed and they were soon on the drive back to the small farm. It seemed so dark at night without any stars or moon, just those darn, strange gray clouds. She parked the car and Alex closed the garage door. As they approached the front steps Aunt Mazer froze. She saw that the front door was open about 4 inches. When she looked through the door window she noticed that the light from the lamp was out and it was laying on the floor. "Alex," she said firmly, "You stay right here!" "No way Aunt Mazer, I'm coming in too." She didn't have time to argue, so they both slowly entered the house. It was so dim and quiet, but then she saw the drawers of her old desk open and everything was scattered on the floor. They made their way toward the kitchen and she took a deep breath. The kitchen screen door was hanging off its hinges and she also saw blood. She opened the small closet next to the door and grabbed the baseball bat she kept there. She felt around for the light switch, and when it lit up the outside she couldn't believe what she was seeing. She started screaming, then Alex saw what she was looking at, and also started screaming so hard he felt sick. "Alex! Alex!. Get to the phone and call the diner right now!" Aunt Mazer screamed. He did just that but was having trouble dialing because he was crying so much. Gerry finally answered the phone, but all she could hear was screaming and Alex trying to talk. She couldn't understand what he was saying, but Gerry knew something terrible had happened at the farm. She dropped the phone and ran out to the counter. She found the guys still sitting at the counter and told them that something horrible had happened at the farm. They were out of the diner in seconds, flying up the road. Willy yelled back, "Call the Sheriff, right now!" As Mazer stood there, she could hear screaming, then realized it was her. She sank down to the floor and started sobbing. Alex was behind her and had buried his face against her back. Again they both looked out the kitchen doorway. Olsen the cat was hanging on the clothesline, with a note tied to the wire around his neck. The heartbreak Mazer felt was unbearable, she then collapsed and passed out. Alex heard car doors slamming so he ran to the front door. He was hysterical and none of the guys could understand him. They all went to the kitchen and found Mazer on the floor. Willy was picking her up when Dave grabbed his shoulder and said, "Oh my God, look!" Willy, being such an animal lover himself felt the same heartbreak. Carl just stared, he was speechless.

Dave started calling Gerry at the diner. Mike answered and told him Gerry and Jeanne were on their way. Mike kept saying, "What happened? What happened?"

Dave told him. Mike couldn't believe it, and Dave could hear others at the diner as they crowded around the phone. Mike told Dave that his mom had just got back. She was still in her fishing clothes when she jumped in her Rover and sped off. Mike's mind was racing, but then he asked Dave if he should call Doc Horton. Dave said, "Yes, yes I didn't even think of that buddy, we'll talk later, I have to go take care of Alex and Mazer."

Mike immediately called the clinic. The girl at the desk answered and put the call right through to Dr. Horton's office. He and the Doctor talked a few minutes. Dr. Horton said he would leave for the farm right away. He grabbed his bag and told his wife Jubilee, who was also a nurse at the clinic what had happened. They both headed for his car. Jubilee kept saying, " God Almighty, what's going to happen next?"

Willy Grey Wolf had laid Mazer on the sofa. Carl and Dave were still standing at the kitchen doorway talking quietly. All of a sudden they jumped as they heard Alex screaming for Cooper. "Damn, I forgot all about the dog" Dave said. Alex flew by them out the door. Carl and Dave were right behind him. They all started calling for Cooper. Finally they heard a bark and saw Cooper come out of the barn. He had some blood on him and was whining a bit. Alex ran to him crying and hugged him. Both Carl and Dave watched, then had Alex walk the dog into the house. None of them wanted to look at the clothesline as they walked in.

They heard several cars pull up and Gerry, Jeanne and Eileen rushed into the house. They also heard a siren and knew Sheriff Lambert would be there in a few minutes.

Mazer was semi-conscious now, but she had curled up on the sofa holding a cushion against her and was sobbing uncontrollably. The girls had rushed over to her, but not before they looked out the kitchen doorway. The Sheriff had just walked in when she heard Eileen angrily talking to Dave and Carl. "This is unbelievable, we have to find out who is doing this!" She slammed her hand on the door frame, then saw the Sheriff and almost pounced on her. "You have to do something" she shouted. "All these horrible incidents are happening for a reason. Nothing was ever found out about Rosie's murder, then all the break ins, now this. What the hell is going on!" Dave knew how angry his mom was so he went over to her trying to calm her down. "Don't tell me to calm down," she shouted "This is bull shit!" The room went quiet and everyone looked at the Sheriff. Eileen started again, this time pacing and mumbling. She looked straight at the Sheriff and said, "Maybe it's time to be hire a Deputy. Something has to be done. I keep thinking whose going to be next? Tell us, do you have any ideas at all about what's going on in this town?" Sheriff Lambert just shook her head. She had been following any kind of leads, but all seemed futile. Eileen's comment about hiring a Deputy was a good idea, but who? She had one person in mind, but kept silent for now.

The front door opened and Dr. Horton and Jubilee hurried in. He went right to Mazer on the sofa and became very concerned. He started to examine her but already was convinced she was in shock. He wanted to take her to the clinic but she just pulled away from him and told him to leave her alone, then again started crying softly.

Uncle Willy went into Alex's bedroom and sat on the bed. Alex was hugging Cooper and would not move. He looked at Uncle Willy and said, " Why would anyone want to hurt Olsen? He was just a big old cat, he never hurt anybody." Alex's eyes were red and swollen from crying so much. He let Uncle Willy check Cooper but he did not find any cuts. The blood on the dog must have been from the intruder Willy thought. He told Alex to lay down, covered him with a quilt and hoped he would sleep for a while with Cooper right by his side.

They were all back in the living room . Dr. Horton had convinced Mazer to take a sedative which made her fall asleep in a few minutes. ,..

Everyone was tense. Dave had taken a large towel from the bathroom and went outside with the Sheriff. "Don't touch the note" she said. She put on a pair of gloves and took the note off Olsen, then Dave carefully cut him down and wrapped him in the towel. Carl and Gerry came out. Dave laid the cat down and went into the barn to find a shovel. He checked on Buttercup and Hannah and found them both huddled in a corner of their stall. "I wish you two could talk" he said. When he came out of the barn he saw Willy talking to the Sheriff. They all looked at the note. It said the same thing as the note left at Rosie's and the What Not Curiosity Shop, "This town is going to die."

Carl had already started to dig a hole for Olsen's grave under one of the Magnolia trees near the barn. He knew Mazer would like that. He also planned on making a simple cross later to mark the grave. Sherriff Lambert put the note in a plastic bag and told them she was going to send it to the State Forensic Lab, hopefully there would be fingerprints on it. Inside, Dr. Horton packed up his medical bag and handed a small bottle with four pills in it to Eileen. He told her the pills were a mild sedative. Eileen nodded and said she was staying, so was Jeanne. Gerry had to go back to the diner to help Mike close up for the night.

Sheriff Lambert was standing next to the cruiser and seemed to be having a serious conversation with Willy Grey Wolf. They all saw he kept nodding his head.

Dr. Horton and Jubilee left, but not before giving Eileen strict instructions. He also wanted her to call him later. Eileen told her son she was staying at Mazer's that night. Carl said he would give Dave a ride back to the Gas N Go.

Willy Grey Wolf had left with Sheriff Lambert. Gerry headed back to the diner, nervous as hell because she knew she had to tell Pinky, but didn't look forward to upsetting her, especially since she was eight months pregnant now.

Jeanne went into Alex's bedroom and saw Alex and Cooper both fast asleep. She turned off his light and went back to the living room. Eileen had covered Mazer with a blanket, then she and Gerry sat in the two recliners next to the sofa. They just looked at each other. No words were spoked as Jeanne simply stared at Eileen. She was rapidly tapping her fingers on the arm of the recliner. Jeanne knew the anger was boiling up in Eileen. She just pushed her recliner back and closed her eyes, knowing it was going to be a long night.

THE TRUE END OF THE THEATRE

She had been driving on the interstate highway for several hours now. Her back was stiff plus she felt weary and tired. Up ahead she saw a Motel 6 and decided to spend the night there instead of driving right through to her destination, which was the small town of Alton.

She parked her Volvo SUV, then entered the main door with just one suitcase, a small carry on that held all the essentials she needed for the night. The desk clerk smiled and welcomed her, saying she was darn lucky because there was only one room available that evening. She smiled back and gave the clerk the necessary ID's, signed in, and then asked, " Just how far is Alton from here?" His mind seemed to wander for a few seconds and then asked her why she was traveling to Alton. He told her it was only about forty miles away. She told him that she had arranged to rent a small theater there. "You know that theater has been closed for quite a while, ever since the Mill fire several years ago." He had a look of concern on his face but she told him that she had heard the entire story of the town and its demise over the years. He seemed genuinely interested and asked if she had family or friends there. She explained to him that she had visited Alton years before, when her sister and brother-in-law had resided there along with their three children. She had loved the little town and was truly saddened when her family left after the massive fire. Her family had to move on to find other employment. That was years ago and she was actually excited to take on the responsibility of the vintage theatre. She had so many plans for it.

She headed to Room 103, unlocked the door and just plopped on the bed. A good night's sleep is what she needed. Her name was Olivia Best, and she was a woman on a mission. Her partner and the love of her life would arrive in Alton the next day.

She had been communicating daily with the small town banker, Charlie Baker, who owned the theatre. Her and Carla, her partner in life, had decided to embark on a new lifestyle. They were tired of big city life and just knew this was a once in a lifetime opportunity for both of them. They had met many years ago while attending the same college. Both of the woman had majored in theatre production, directing, projection engineering and thoroughly enjoyed the aspect of old movies. They were older now and deeply connected. When Olivia heard that the old theatre was still in good condition, she and Carla thought it might help bring life again to the dwindling town. They were so excited. Money was not an issue with either of them, so they both looked forward to this challenging endeavor. Carla had found a restoration company and also a reputable cleaning company. That part of the enterprise had already started the day before. Olivia looked at the bedside clock. She had to be up and on her way to Alton by 9AM. Her anticipation was overwhelming, but she finally fell asleep with so many plans dancing in her dreams that night.

The next morning she had already spoken with Carla. Charlie the banker had also informed them that there was a lovely apartment above the theatre itself.

Even before Olivia reached Alton, many of the towns people had noticed the comings and goings of painters, an electrician and a plumber.

There were only sixty seats in the theatre, but the carpeting, tile floor and two restrooms were in excellent condition. Olivia had been concerned about a musty odor but the cleaning company had proved to be more than adequate after they had completed their job.

As usual, the news spread about the re-opening of the theatre. Charlie the banker had hired Benny to repaint the ornate sign above the entrance doorway and Olivia had chosen a dark turquoise which actually seemed to bring life to the brick building.

Her Volvo was packed with numerous tins of 8MM vintage movies. She and Carla had collected most of their favorites over the years. Casablanca, Rear Window, Singing in the Rain and On the Beach were just some of them, along with quite a few old horror movies which they hoped would be favorites for many of the towns people. Carla was an expert projectionist, while Olivia would handle the financial end of the business. This had been their plan all along.

As Olivia drove closer to the town line of Alton the next morning, she noticed the odd cloud formations. She relished in the thought of seeing a crowded theatre again in the small town. A quiet time with popcorn and snacks would definitely draw the people of Alton just so they could enjoy a much needed change.

The two women had wanted to schedule the grand opening as soon as possible. All the towns people were curious, especially Carl, Arnie and the Big Four, (Mazer, Eileen, Gerry and Jeanne). Little did they know that evil was also looking forward to making his appearance at the Alton Theatre.

Olivia and Carla were so astonished when many people stopped by to wish them well. They had been a bit nervous because of their lesbian relationship, but found that their concerns didn't matter at all. They felt welcomed and at ease, even from the local Sheriff, Officer Lambert. They had been cornered by old man Sydney as he walked his dog and prevailed them of the town's history. Boy that old man could talk. They made some excuses about being so busy with the opening of the theatre and quietly laughed as they crossed the street quickly. The two women had planned to have a personal opening rehearsal, so they were in a rush anyway to get back to the theatre.

They sat in two of the plush theatre seats, looked at each other and kissed. They hadn't felt this excited in years. All of a sudden they noticed the lights dimming and discussed calling the electrician in the morning. They were both still a bit tired and knew there was so much to do before their grand opening for the towns people.

Carla got up and headed toward the projection room. Olivia told her she needed to visit the restroom and would soon meet her at their special seats again. Carla kept checking the sound system, and priming the projection machine. Both women had decided to sit in the refurbished theatre and watch one of their favorite movies, 'Imitation of Life' for their own debut and revel in their new success. They had just made microwave popcorn and had two soda's with them. They didn't want to start up the concession stand yet for just the two of them, although the cases of popcorn and the boxes of assorted candy had already been delivered that morning. The soda machines had been tested and were ready to go. They both had dressed up for their special theatre affair and were actually in a romantic mood that evening. They hadn't planned on any previews, so as the movie started they held hands. After the credits, they totally enjoyed watching the classic acting of Lana Turner, John Gavin and Sandra Dee.

All of a sudden the theatre went totally dark. The movie was still playing, but that was the only illumination in the theatre at that time. "God dammit" Carla said as she stood up and headed to the area where the circuit breakers were located. All of a sudden the audio of the movie stopped also. Olivia continued to just sit and nervously munched on her popcorn. She felt a chill go up her spine and anxiously waited for Carla. She turned and called Carla's name but there was no response. Carla had always been the stronger of the pair and Olivia hoped that they would both soon be laughing about this. She felt like she was viewing a silent movie when she suddenly froze, because just then the screen went dark also. She slowly rose from her seat and looked up toward the projection room. That area was also completely dark. She stood up and cautiously felt her way up the aisle and then saw a dark figure standing before her. "We are not officially open yet" she said. The dark figure limped toward her and she saw that he had a large knife in one hand. She screamed but no one heard her as the blade of the knife cut right across her throat. She didn't even have the chance to see Carla's body lying in the aisle right behind the dark figure. About fifteen minutes later, the movie reappeared on the screen again with the two women sitting beside each other in the front row. The only difference was that the appearance of Carla and Olivia had been changed. Their heads were now placed on the opposite of each other's bodies. Their blood coated several of the movie seats and the popcorn they had been eating littered the aisle. This movie premier had been planned to be like no other. A note was placed on the movie screen pasted with blood so it would be noticed immediately. Like all the other messages found, it said, "This town is going to die!"

There had been no activity at the theatre, and people began to notice and ask questions. The Grand Opening, according to the flyers that had been distributed around town was supposed to be on Friday evening, which was the next day. The glass doors were still covered with paper, and there had been no lights on at all. Even Sheriff Lambert became concerned. No one had seen the two women and their cars were still parked on the side of the theater, as though Olivia and Carla were still unloading supplies.

Late Thursday evening, Sheriff Lambert and Willy Grey Wolf decided to visit the theatre to ask the women if they needed help in any way, which gave them an excuse to make sure everything was okay. The doors to the lobby of the small theatre were unlocked which the Sheriff and Willy found very strange. Her and Willy Grey Wolf opened the heavy doors to the main part of the theatre, and was surprised to see a movie playing, but there was no sound at all. Willy clicked on his large flashlight and began scanning all the seats and aisles. He stopped when he saw the two women sitting in the front row. They seemed to be staring at the large screen. He waited for Sheriff Lambert as she exited the ladies room. "All clear in there," she said, but did not move when she saw what Willy was shining his light on. They walked down the aisle toward the two women, then the Sheriff called out to them, "Olivia, Carla, are you ok?" They continued to walk down the aisle, but as they came closer there was a peculiar odor. Willy just looked at the Sheriff. She put her hand on Olivia's shoulder and went to shake it lightly. She almost jumped four feet in the air as Olivia's head tipped over and rolled down thc aisle of the theatre. Sheriff Lambert let out a scream, looked at Willy and said, "Another one, I can't do this anymore." She actually felt faint. Willy continued to look at the two corpses, then nudged the Sheriff. She looked at what he was shining his light on this time and sure enough, the same note, "This town is going to die" was placed in plain sight attached to the movie screen with the edges covered in blood. "I think it's time for more help," Willy said, as he pushed the Sheriff out of the building. Now, while they were standing outside in front of the main doors, Willy made sure the latch for the heavy lock was engaged. They both looked at each other in a bewildered way. Sheriff Lambert and Willy Grey Wolf quickly headed for her office. Unfortunately both of them had become too accustomed to the police procedures that were once again needed.

CPL ELI-THE MARINE

Eli and the other Marines were in a C-130 being flown to Camp Leatherneck in Afghanistan. He had slept for a while, but was now eating a couple of protein bars and drinking a bottle of spring water. Next to him was his good friend Roger Elison, fast asleep. They were already 5 hours into a 15 hour flight. This was Eli's second tour of duty and had flown frequently, so he was aware of the intermittent turbulence, the loud snoring of the other Marines and the many hours of boredom. Camp Leatherneck is the home base of most of the U.S. Marine Corps in Afghanistan. It is a military powerhouse now, even though it had begun as a barren outpost in 2009. He didn't know exactly what the assignment was yet, but did know that they would be in the Helmond Province. It was a desolate country with temperatures sometimes reaching 135 degrees. He was part of the 5Th Marine Regiment, one of the most highly decorated ones.

He took out one of his bags that he had been using as a pillow. He kept all the letters in there from home. He remembered he had a new letter from Pinky since they were given all their mail before they boarded for the long flight. He knew every letter from her because they came in a pink envelope of course, which always made Eli smile. He opened the envelope and a picture fell out. He picked it up and kept turning it around and finally realized what it was and shouted, "Holy Crap." He just stared at the small photo. Roger and a few other Marines woke up when they heard Eli's shout. There was a lot of stretching, yawning and murmurs as many of them looked at Eli. Roger looked at him and said, "Hey Eli, thanks for waking me up, I was having this great dream about a little blonde stripper I know." "I'm sorry, I'm sorry" Eli said, then he showed the picture to Roger. Roger was still rubbing his eyes as he leaned over towards Eli. "God damn, that's a sonogram!" "Yea, I know," said Eli. "I just figured that out buddy." He stared at the photo again then read the letter that was with it::

> My dearest Eli, I miss you so much. I hope you are staying safe. I've enclosed this picture as a big surprise for you. I didn't want to tell you before you left. I hope you're not upset. The sonogram shows our sweet baby girl. Imagine, we're going to be parents. I feel great and have been so busy with work and my sewing. Benny from the hardware store came over and brought paint samples for the babies room. Of course it will be in shades of pink. Aunt Mazer, Eileen, Jeanne and Gerry have been planning a baby shower. They think I don't know about it, but I bribed Alex with his favorite pie and he easily spilled the beans. Please don't worry, I know you'll be home before we know it. I already picked out a name, I hope you don't mind, but I know you'll love it. It's Charlotte Pearl. Things here in town have been a bit strange. There has been quite a few break ins and old Rosie (Ms. Cranky Pants) was murdered. There still hasn't been any rain, and people are worried, especially the farmers. Everyone asks about you all the time and they all send their love. Well, I have to get to the diner. I'm putting in as many hours as possible and saving a lot of money. Our new "little guest" is going to be needing

a lot of diapers. Don't worry, Gerry is giving me a lot of light duty and watching over me like a Mother Hen. We have such a great bunch of people here. We are blessed and I am so happy. Please write soon, I love you so much.

Hugs and kisses to you,

Your Pinky

Eli read the letter three times and had a jerky smile on his face. Roger was passing the sonogram photo around, and of course Eli laughed when all the guys started whooping and hollering. His Lieutenant had heard the news and said, "Congratulations Daddy" and laughed. He told him he had better get some sleep before they landed in a few hours, but Eli was so excited and his mind was racing. Roger was snoring away and all the Marines on the plane had quieted down again. Eli laid his head back down and did manage to fall asleep, dreaming of pink dragon flies-Pinky's favorite. The skies were cloudy and the heat hit them like opening a door to a furnace when they had finally landed at the base in the Helmond Province, Afghanistan at 0600. It was a fairly modern facility now in that area.

After unloading their gear in one of the small compounds, the only thing on their minds at that time was a good breakfast, which they knew would be their last big meal for a while. Once they left on their mission, it would be MRE's, protein bars and lots of water.

They were chowing down on eggs, bacon, sausage, flapjacks, biscuits, different kinds of fruit and lots of coffee. Small talk was going on and Eli was still getting ribbed about becoming a new daddy. He didn't mind, though he could hardly believe it. While they were at breakfast the talk turned to the heat outside. It was hot and one of the Marines said it was expected to reach 110 degrees that day. Just all the gear itself was over 100 lbs. Another Marine said a Lance Cpl. had come up with an idea on how to keep their water cool. Bottles of hot water were put in a cotton sock then soaked in well water and hung out to let the wind dry it. In an hour or two it was like taking the bottles right out of a refrigerator. It worked and really helped, especially when walking through waist high fields of opium poppies. Small talk continued, but all Eli could think about was Pinky and the new baby. He kept the sonogram picture in the left pocket of his inside shirt, along with a 100 year old Silver dollar that Uncle Willy had given him for good luck. It had been his Dads, and both were now close to his heart.

After breakfast, they were ordered to report to the main compound. They knew they were going to be briefed about the special assignment. So many of the Marines had their own suspicions and after saluting the Commanding Officer and taking a seat when told, "at ease" the room became as quiet as a church. The mission was explained and discussed but the orders still seemed somewhat vague. They were told to be ready in two hours. After all were dismissed they headed for their compound and started preparing. Eli had been gone for weeks now and was feeling a bit homesick. Suck it up he told himself, this was going to be a very short but special assignment and he knew that he soon would be back on that big old plane heading for home. That thought made him feel better, but before long he was reaching for his helmet and quickly walking to all the vehicles waiting outside with 11 other Marines.

Eli was riding in the last vehicle, a Humvee. There were two large supply trucks in front of them that had been fully loaded and secured. The first vehicle was another Humvee, with four Marines in that one also. All they had been told was that they were delivering special weapons, ammunition and other supplies to a small village about 90 miles away. Rumor had it that it evidently had been a Taliban stronghold but was successfully taken by a larger Marine Unit about 3 weeks ago. Right now they were just trying to stabilize that entire area. His good friend Roger was driving the last Humvee. He was softly whistling a tune and Eli smiled, knowing that he was still probably thinking of that little blonde stripper he had dreamt about. Eli was checking his weapon, a Benelli M-4 Super 90. He loved his gun. It reminded him of the shotgun his Dad taught him how to use when he was young, but of course this weapon was much more sophisticated. The two Marines in the back seat had M-16 A-4 rifles, as did Roger, along with his holstered pistol.

It took the small unit just a little over two hours to reach their destination. The town was called Magrims, and it seemed to be a quiet area. The 24th Marine Expeditionary Unit had captured Magrims from the Taliban after a month of constant battle. This was in the southern district of Afghanistan and the heat was almost unbearable. One Marine said it was even too hot for mosquito's. Only 200 Marines remained there. They were living in crude mud wall compounds. There was no sewage or regular telephones, but many generators were being operated for much needed electricity. After they parked the vehicles they realized what a welcome sight they were for the Marines that were camped there. Roger told Eli that he had seen two large mail bags in the back of the first Humvee. He knew just how crucial it was for the Marines moral to be able to receive letters and packages from back home in the U.S., and once again he thought of Pinky's last letter. It was going to be dusk soon. Only the last Humvee with Roger, Eli and the other two Marines would be returning to Camp Leatherneck that evening.

After many handshakes and even some bear hugs, the four Marines returned to their Humvee. As their vehicle was pulling away, a Marine named Tony was running toward them carrying a large mail bag. "Almost forgot to give this to you guys. Glad I caught you before you started back." Tony stuffed the mail bag in the trunk of the Humvee and waved goodbye to all of them.

As they drove on it seemed so quiet. The land was nothing but sand, dirt and stone, desolate in its own way. About 50 yards up ahead, Eli thought he had spotted two figures walking on the right side of the road. He glanced at Roger, then at the two Marines sitting in the back. Craig, the older of the two in the back seat, was staring out the side window and said, "I already saw them." Eli heard two clicks from the back seat and knew the two Marines had unlocked their safeties from their rifles.

Roger sat back a bit and unsnapped his holster, his M-9 Barretta was now right at his fingertips. Raley, the other Marine in the back seat then said, "I think I see a third one walking also, but about 50 feet to the right of the other two." Sure enough, Eli and the others now saw the third figure. As they were driving closer the two figures walking together looked to be only young boys dressed in traditional Afghan smocks. They had stopped and seemed to be waving at the Marines, and shouting something in their Dari language. "Looks just like kids," Roger said, "but I'm still not stopping." The others agreed and were steadily keeping a keen watch on all of them. Just as the Humvee was about to pass them, Eli thought they were throwing rocks at them, but then realized what was happening. "Grenades," he screamed. Roger had slammed on the brakes, but it was too late. The Humvee had driven right over three grenades, and the next thing Eli felt was the vehicle becoming airborne and rolling four times before it landed on its roof. There was the smell of fuel and another explosion. The screams from the back seat were deafening. Eli fumbled for his seatbelt and unsnapped it. He reached over for Rogers and did the same. He also grabbed Rogers pistol then he started to kick out the windshield. He had to get Roger out. He was not responding, but Eli hoped he was only unconscious. He finally managed to kick out the front window and started dragging Rogers limp body through it. He felt his dog tags catch on something and rip away from his neck. He was limping badly but continued to pull Roger as far away from the Humvee as he could. He saw one of the boys running toward him, screaming something. Eli raised the pistol that he had retrieved from Rogers holster and shot the screaming boy in the forehead. He could hear the other two and quickly covered Roger with his own body. He now saw the other two running toward him. He fired off two more rounds and watched as one of them spun around and fell to the ground. One more he said to himself, and all of a sudden felt hands around his neck. The third boy seemed to be acting wildly, grabbing for his neck and even Rogers neck. Eli rolled over quickly and kicked him in the face as hard as he could. The boy fell back and that gave Eli just the seconds he needed to fire two more rounds into his chest. He laid back for a few seconds, then crawled over to Roger. He kept calling his name, but there was no response. He could feel blood dripping down his own face and his left arm felt heavy, with a sharp pain in his left shoulder. Must be shrapnel he thought. He also saw blood around Rogers neck and felt some deep wounds around his own neck. He looked back at the third boy and saw that he had a small knife in his hand. He checked for a pulse on Roger, but he already knew he was dead. That's when the tears started, then he just passed out, still holding Rogers pistol. He thought he was dreaming, when he felt light rain on his face. It appeared to be very light out and he wondered how long he had been unconscious. He heard distant voices. He tried to raise his hand that had the pistol in it, but he couldn't. He was so tired, he just closed his eyes. Again he thought he was dreaming as he heard a voice calling, "Eli, Eli." He slowly opened his eyes and saw several Marines. He gave a small smile of relief and tried to speak. The medic kneeling over him told him not to talk. "You'll be ok, I promise." He felt himself being lifted and was placed on a stretcher. They then pushed the stretcher into a Medic van. He felt more aware now and looked around. Two Humvees were there and several Marines stood guard around the vehicles. There was a shout and one of the Marines said, "I just saw two more figures near those stones to the left." He heard gunfire then someone said that they ran over the ridge, and the gunfire ceased.

He saw the Medic was a woman. She had short curly blonde hair and stood only 5 feet tall, but still wore the full Marine uniform, except for a cross of Red on her sleeve and on her chest. She had a great smile and as she asked him his name, he closed his eyes and said, "Eli, my name is Eli." He looked at her again and saw she was starting an IV in his uninjured arm. "Well bless my heart," she replied in a distinct Southern drawl. "My name is Ellen, but everyone calls me Eli, and it's spelled the same way." She chuckled, then said, "I'm going to give you something for the pain, so just relax and enjoy the ride back to base. After your condition is stabilized, you'll be going home Marine. You lost quite a bit of blood, but you'll be just fine. You sure are lucky." She smiled at him and then added, "Your Angel was sure looking after you." Eli closed his eyes as he felt himself drifting away, and just thought of Pinky with a slight smile on his face.

He felt he was coming in and out of his sleep phase. All of a sudden he remembered the Mail Bag. He whispered, "The Mail Bag, the Mail Bag!" The little blonde Medic came to his side, and patted his arm. "Don't worry, one of the Marines found it about 20 yards from the vehicle. Evidently it had been blown out from the back of the Humvee when the grenades went off. It was a bit singed, but other than that the bag was intact. Go back to sleep, we'll be back at Camp Leatherneck soon." He fell back to sleep, but about an hour later he could hear many voices and the sound of boots on the ground. Several Medics were shouting orders, and another Medic Van pulled up. He saw that four Marines were removing the bodies of the three who had been killed. They would be taken to a small Quonset hut which was refrigerated. This particular building was well known to all the Marines there. It was referred to as the 'silent zone" and all the Marines who passed by the hut always stopped and saluted, out of respect for their fallen brothers.

Eli was carried by stretcher into the hospital facility at the base. As he was carefully placed onto one of the empty beds, a Dr. was there immediately to evaluate his condition. He was starting a new chart while taking a report from the Medic who had traveled back with him. The Dr. was checking him all over as two nurses carefully removed his uniform. "Well, not too bad," he said. "Multiple contusions and bruises. His left ankle seems to have a severe sprain, but we'll x-ray it to make sure there is no fracture. His left shoulder has a three inch piece of shrapnel embedded in it also. He's going to need sutures there and also on the deep laceration he has on his scalp." Eli was conscious now, so the Dr. did a thorough exam for any kind of concussion or other head trauma. The Dr. looked at him and said, "We're going to patch you up just fine. You won't be fit for any duty for quite a while, so I'm going to recommend that you be shipped home as soon as possible. You've earned it." Eli tried to relax, but then remembered his shirt. He shouted, "My shirt, my shirt, I need it for a minute." One of the nurses handed it to him and he was so relieved when he pulled out the silver dollar and the sonogram photo. "Anything else?" the nurse said. "No, no, that's all and thank you so much, I really mean it." It did not even enter his mind that he didn't have his dog tags on. He then went back to sleep.

In the Quonset hut where the bodies of the three dead soldiers were, stood a Marine who was straight out of boot camp. His name was Antwone and had only arrived three days before. He was determined to become a top notch Medic, but today he would make a mistake that would follow him forever.

He put gloves on and slowly unzipped each body bag. The first two bodies were the Marines that had been severely burned. He checked the clip board and noticed their dog tags had been actually embedded into their chests, but luckily were still recordable. He only had to place the wristbands on them for proper identification.

He saw a small box on one of the stainless steel tables. It was marked, 'personal property.' He knew it had come from the attack site. He picked up the box and dumped all the contents onto the table. He had to list everything according to military policy, so as he held the clip board he started that chore. There were two Zippo lighters that had the Marine Corps emblem on them, two wallets badly burned, three packs of gum that were melted, a handful of assorted coins and a set of dog tags. He checked the identification on the dog tags, then carefully unzipped the third body bag. There was quite a bit of dried blood, especially around the Marines neck, but no dog tags. He checked the dog tags again and the name on them was Eli Rosker. He placed them in the pocket of the dead soldiers shirt, but left the broken chain hanging out so it would be visible. He labeled the final toe tag and wrist band with Eli Rosker's name on them and then zipped up the body bag. Little did he know that the dog tags belonging to Roger Elison had slipped down and was actually under his body. All three of the bodies were scheduled to be shipped back to the states the next day. He felt a sadness as he knew what the next procedure would be. A two man team would be notifying the families within twenty four hours. He bowed his head in reverence, turned and left the Quonset hut, locking it securely.

After three days Eli was getting very restless. He was walking around the wards with crutches, but still had sutures in his shoulder and scalp. The multiple bruises all over him were still visible, and they had also found that his ribs were damaged because three of them on the left side had small hairline fractures. This didn't stop Eli though. Every day he hounded his Dr. about being released on medical leave. He even started to follow the Dr. while he made his rounds. "Hey Doc, when am I going to get out of here? Tell me, just tell me when please?" The Dr. never gave him a definite answer, just always said, "A few more days, be patient, you still have sutures in."

Today he was hunting down some paper, a pen and a couple of envelopes. He had been putting it off but was going to write Roger Elison's family a letter. He and Roger had been friends since childhood. They both loved football, target shooting, hunting with their dads, and girls. Oh the girls. Roger was a handsome boy and never had a problem with the girl issue. Eli remembered how they would 'borrow' one of their dad's trucks and drive through all the logging trails. One day they were sitting on a large flat stone near a small pond in the forest. As they took turns skipping stones, Roger told him the plans he had for himself. "I'm not getting married until I'm thirty. I don't want to be tied down. I want to travel and see the world. I might even enlist in the military just so I can do that." Roger looked at Eli and smiled. "No offense buddy, but I'm not like you. I know you and Pinky are meant for each other. You both will get married and have a great family, while I send you post cards from all over the world." They both laughed then headed for home. A few months after the terrible Mill fire, his family had been one of the unfortunates that had to move. They settled in another small town that was quickly growing. It was about eighty miles away, but Eli and Roger kept in close contact through the years. They had even enlisted together and knew they would be the closest of friends for life.

Eli felt teary eyed as he thought of this, knowing Roger would never be able to follow his dreams now. He had lost his best friend and remained sullen as he wrote a letter to Roger's family.

The second letter was to Pinky. He was going to tell her what happened, and that he would be home soon. He wrote that he promised he would be with her when the new baby came into their world. He felt better when he was licking the envelopes and would make sure they were mailed out the next day, which unfortunately never happened as planned.

Almost another week passed. Eli spent his time playing cards or dominos with another Marine he had become friends with. It helped pass the time. He gave up hounding the Dr. and nurses about when he was going to be released.

All of a sudden he saw the Dr. and head nurse walking toward his bed. The Dr. was reading Eli's chart while walking, but the nurse was smiling and even gave him a wink and thumbs up. She was carrying a suture removal kit, a package of gloves and some paper work. The Dr. just stood there and continued to look at his chart. He finally put the chart down and said, "Well, I think today's the day." Before Eli could respond the Dr. started to tell him what the plan was. Eli was smiling, he could hardly sit still. The Dr. started by explaining to him that he was going to remove the sutures, do a short basic exam and then tomorrow fill out all the necessary paper work for his medical leave. But he said, and Eli held his breath, "One of the rehab technicians also had to check him out tomorrow and verify that he was ready to leave." "Sound like a plan?" said the Dr. Eli smiled and started to reply, when the Dr. said, "You should be out of here in about three days." Eli knew it was futile to argue about the three days, and just stayed quiet while they started to check his wounds again. He felt better when they were finished, and started to think about Pinky and going home. He would sleep well tonight even though he was excited. Going home, holding Pinky again, and seeing all his friends and especially Aunt Mazer and Alex. He closed his eyes and took a well needed nap.

CARL'S BIG MOVE

Carl was an early riser, and this morning at the shop he had so much on his mind. For some time now he had been seriously thinking about buying old Rosie's property. He even called her nephew who lived in one of the larger cities inland. Carl knew there had been no interested buyers, and that the house was small and needed updating. Last night he finally decided to do it. For years he had lived in the small loft above the butcher shop. He knew it was time to take that big step with Sheriff Lambert. He adored her and he knew the feeling was mutual. He had never really been involved in any serious relationships through the years. Any other women tended to be intimidated because of his Tourette's Syndrome. Not Sheriff Lambert though. She actually seemed to be able to calm him down when he needed it most.

Bennie from the hardware store walked through the small house with Carl and Willy Grey Wolf. Carl had made a list of changes he wanted, like tearing up the old carpets and refurbishing the floors, and Bennie thoroughly agreed. The house had been cleared out after Rosie's murder and then professionally cleaned. The kitchen was in excellent condition, as was the bathroom. Bennie had checked the wiring and the plumbing and informed Carl that only some minor repairs needed to be done.

Carl had spoken twice with the nephew and they had haggled about the price at first. The nephew knew this was a great opportunity especially since no one else had been interested in buying the small house. He realized that the price Carl was offering was a bit less, but a smaller amount was better than nothing. The deal was made. Carl had always been financially disciplined and already had the money. The nephew made the trip down to Alton with a friend who was a real estate lawyer. The closing procedure was completed and the nephew handed Carl the keys. Good luck he said. Afterward Carl stood in the living room. The couch, recliner and two end tables had been left, and remained covered. He knew that Rosie had purchased the set almost brand new from a family that had moved two years before. He uncovered everything and was elated to see that the entire set of furniture were like brand new.

He had hired Willy Grey Wolf and two of his friends to paint the outside of the house. It was going to be light gray with white trim. He was also going to add white shutters on all the windows. He was going to re-do the living room and bedroom floors. There was a slight breeze today, so he had opened most of the windows to air the house out. Carl was a simple man so he didn't have much to move from the loft. He smiled as he thought the Sheriff couldn't complain anymore about the meat smell that many times wafted up from the vents in the butcher shop. He also was fully aware that the towns people would be gossiping away when he and Sheriff Lambert moved in together. He didn't mind because he knew just about all of them would be happy for the couple. He loved the idea that he could even walk to the butcher shop from the house, because it was less than two blocks away. He locked up the house and started back to his place. He looked up at the sky and noticed those strange gray rippled clouds, but even that couldn't change his great mood as he walked down the street whistling and smiling to himself.

He looked at his watch, it was 10:30AM. He was in the small supply closet at the butcher shop when he heard the bell ring as the front door opened, then banged shut. He thought it must be an early customer, which was unusual during the week. He washed his hands and were wiping them as he went into the front of the store. His mouth just about fell open because he couldn't believe who he saw. It was his nephew, Wayne Swenson, carrying a medium sized suitcase in his left hand. Wayne dropped the suitcase and shouted, "Uncle Carl, aren't you glad to see me?" Wayne looked around and said, "Wow, this place hasn't changed much. What's new, how have you been? I guess you didn't hear about my Dad. Can I sit down, you got any coffee?" He grabbed a freshly baked scone and starting munching away, while walking around the store and looking at everything. "Well speak up man, what's it been, about 13 years since we last saw each other?" Carl just looked at Wayne, who was about four years older than him. Time had not been kind to him. He had put on quite a bit of weight and was missing several of his teeth. Even his blonde hair had a bit of silver in it now. Carl smiled and said, "Just surprised to see you, sure, have a seat. What happened to your Dad? Why are you here ?" Wayne grabbed a chair and another scone. Carl was already getting aggravated. "Well," Wayne started, "Dad passed away about three months ago. He had married again while living in Florida. She got everything, if you know what I mean. I had meant to call you with the news, then the small butcher shop I was managing went under. Such a shame. I got nothing, Uncle Carl. Even had to sell my old car just for bus fare to come here." Now he started to cry a bit as he grabbed a third scone. Carl moved the tray of scones and placed it under the counter. "I thought I could work for you, even if it was just part-time. You know I have always had a knack for the butcher business."

"I don't know what to say Wayne" Carl replied. He felt the Tourette's Syndrome trying to take over his speech, so he kept as silent as possible. He did remember he agreed to look after Wayne if anything had happened to Wayne's father, but never thought about it again.. Now this is a predicament, he thought. "Well Wayne, we'll have to have a serious talk about all this. I was just heading out to the diner for lunch." "Great" Wayne said, "you can buy me lunch."

Carl put Wayne's suitcase in the back and then they started walking to the diner. Wayne was looking up at the sky. He took off his jacket then said, “Boy, it’s really humid here, and what’s with those damn weird clouds? I could see them about ten miles out.” He kept talking, “This town is so quiet, almost looks like a ghost town. What do people do for fun here? I’ve never seen so many empty houses.” Carl wasn’t a big talker, he just told him that they were having a bit of a drought, that’s all.

They walked in the diner and Carl was already dreading the stares. “Hi everyone, this is my cousin Wayne, visiting from out of town.” There it was, the stutter. Wayne looked at him and mockingly said, “Still got that stutter and all ? I sure thought you would have grown out of that.” Now Carl was getting a bit hot under the collar. They sat in a booth and ordered lunch. Gerry came by and gave Carl an odd look and greeted Wayne. While they ate, Carl was deep in thought. Wayne could stay in the loft. He could work part-time, but he would have to make sure Wayne knew it was only going to be temporary. Carl had never wanted any employee’s. Later that day they made a deal. The next day some of the guys from town helped Carl move his things to the new house. He would paint while living there now. In fact, with Wayne working a few hours at the shop, it would give Carl more time to renovate the small house. He sighed when he thought that it just might work in his favor. He didn’t care for his cousin that much, never did. He decided he was going to keep his distance, and hoped the new plan would work out. That next day, he told Sheriff Lambert all about it. She laughed so hard she almost peed her pants, She met Wayne, and then she totally understood where Carl was coming from.

BACK AT THE FARM

It was about 9AM when Eileen and Jeanne woke up. The house was so still and quiet. The only sound was from the chickens clucking outside. They both yawned and looked at the sofa, it was empty. Mazer was not there. They quickly walked to the smaller bedroom, opened the door a bit and saw Alex and Cooper still sleeping. Then they checked Mazer's bedroom and saw that it was empty, the bed still neatly made.

There had been an incident about 2:30 AM. Mazer suddenly woke up and became frantic, and began screaming again. Eileen knew she saw rage in Mazer's face. Mazer began pacing the room and slamming her fists on the furniture. She even grabbed the telephone next to the sofa and threw it into the kitchen, wires and all. Jeanne ran for a glass of water and between the two of them they made Mazer swallow another sedative that Doc Horton had left with them. They finally calmed her down enough so she would lay on the sofa. They both felt better after Mazer fell asleep again.

Now that it was morning and Mazer was no longer on the sofa, they both looked at each other. They quietly walked to the kitchen doorway, noticing again that only splinters of wood remained there. Mazer was sitting on the ground next to Olsen's grave. Jeanne started to call to her, but Eileen grabbed her arm and said, "Let her be, I think she needs some quiet time, I really do."

Jeanne started a pot of coffee while Eileen continued to keep watch at the kitchen doorway. They both heard soft footsteps and turned to see Alex with Cooper right behind them. He looked half asleep and his eyes were still swollen and red a bit. "I'm hungry" Alex said, then also added that he had to feed Coop and let him out. "Can I have a bowl of Cheerios?" "Of course you can sweetie" Jeanne replied. "Sit down and I'll get it for you." While Jeanne got a bowl, spoon, milk, and the box of cereal, Eileen let Cooper out, but sure enough he spotted Mazer and ran to her. Jeanne heard a vehicle pull up out front and went to see who it was. A big white van with "Carl's Butcher Shop" painted on the side of it was parked in the gravel driveway. Carl had taken something out of the back of the van and was walking around to the far right side of the house. In one hand he carried a sand stake and hammer, and in the other hand was a well- made white cross. He walked up to Mazer, who started crying again. All she kept saying was "I just can't believe it" and she hugged Carl. She saw a small silver plaque on the middle of the cross and printed in neat letters it said, "Olsen the Cat." She thanked him over and over, then stood and watched while Carl set the cross firmly in the ground where Olsen was buried. They both walked back to the kitchen and carefully went through the doorway. Carl told Mazer that Willy Grey Wolf would be by tomorrow to replace the kitchen door. Mazer looked so tired and drawn. She kissed Alex on the forehead and went into the living room and sat on the sofa. Eileen still thought Mazer was in a state of shock and would keep a close eye on her, plus she had promised to call Doc Horton that afternoon.

Carl left. He told them that he was meeting Willy Grey Wolf, Dave, Bennie and Arnie up at the Great House. He promised they would stop here after they did their own investigation.

Eileen told Jeanne she was going back to her house to change, plus stop at the clinic and talk with Doc Horton. She couldn't use the telephone at the farm and her cell phone was dead because she had forgotten to charge it. She knew Jeanne would be fine. She had always admired how strong a woman she was. Mazer seemed to be sleeping again, so Eileen got in her Rover and drove off. She told Jeanne that she would be back in about an hour or so.

Just as Eileen returned, the guys also arrived. They stood around the kitchen talking softly. "We didn't find a thing," Dave said. "Not even any footprints." Arnie just shook his head saying it was very strange being up there. Eileen put her hands on her hips, showing an angry kind of authority. "Well, I know Mazer did not imagine seeing a light in one of the top windows all those times!" "No, I didn't!" They all turned around and stared at Mazer. Alex had just come back from the barn after feeding Buttercup and Hannah. He went to his room with Cooper and closed his door. "He's afraid, and so am I." said Mazer. "Something bad is going on in this town." She looked at all of them and said "I'm feeling better, all I want right now is some peace and quiet. I don't need babysitting, please." They all understood and hugged her. Willy told her he would bring the replacement door tomorrow and he asked Eileen to call the telephone company as he looked at the broken phone on the kitchen floor. "Sorry about that," Mazer said. "I was just not myself last night." "No apologies necessary," Jeanne replied, "But do me one favor Mazer, please make sure you eat something, ok?" Jeanne was still concerned, but they all left within 20 minutes. Mazer had fibbed because she did feel scared, furious and depressed. She closed her eyes and asked her "Magic Guy in the Sky" to help her bring things back to some degree of normalcy, especially for Alex. She laid back down on the sofa, but all she could think of was her Olsen.

THE PAINTING PARTY

Carl's store was open until 7PM on Thursday's. He had left Wayne there with detailed instructions concerning his new duties at the butcher shop. "Hey Cous, don't worry, I got this." Wayne said. Those words were supposed to reassure Carl, but he still had doubts about his cousin. Then Carl thought, what could happen? I'll only be a little over a block away. He had told Wayne that it could get busy. Quite a few of the towns people did their meat shopping before the weekend. A large order of baby-back ribs was ready for pickup. One of his usual customers had called it in, explaining that his family was having a big cookout Friday night. He had also prepared an order of thick cut pork cutlets for the two Nuns from the small rectory. Twice a month they treated themselves and always came by on a Thursday evening. He thought about the Nuns and chuckled. They didn't drive, but instead they rode their stylish Schwinn bicycles all over town. Dave had even attached carry baskets on the front of their bicycles for them. They always made him smile, especially since the Nuns didn't cringe when he had one of his Tourette's episodes. He made sure that Wayne knew their order was already packaged and labeled in the refrigerator.

Arnie and Bennie were both coming over to help Carl paint the ceilings early that evening. Benny told Carl he would bring the beer. He knew what that meant, they'd be putting back a few while singing old rock songs. He felt it was going to be a long, loud night, but he greatly appreciated all their help. Carl was anxious to move his antique brass bed into the new house. He also had an antique bureau, two night stands and a chest of drawers that had been in his family for over sixty five years. He loved antiques and could often be found browsing through the new 'finds' at the What Not Curiosity Shop after the twins returned from one of their antique fairs. Also, with the new color that Sheriff Lambert picked out for the walls, the bedroom would look wonderful. Even though the new house was small, it would be so much better than the cramped loft he had lived in for years. The Sheriff was excited also, she would even have her own closet.

Carl put some chips and dip out. He then started covering the furniture with the large sheets of plastic he had bought at the hardware store. He had everything ready. Paint rollers, tape, brushes and a small cooler with ice for the beer. He put the radio on, turned up the volume and started to sing along to an old Rolling Stones song.

Part Five

THE HITCH HIKER

Walking down a quiet country road at night did not really bother the hitch hiker, what bothered the boy the most was the strange clouds that never seemed to move. The hitch hiker was also wearing a long dark coat and carrying a backpack that was black. It made him seem almost invisible. There had been no form of traffic on either side of the road. Only the sound of animals running through the forest from time to time.

It felt as though he had been walking for days, even though it had been only about five hours. He was headed to his sister's house which was about two hours outside of Alton. He could see some lights far off in the distance now, so he knew he was getting closer to the town limits.

He had started counting his steps to break the boredom and then remembered the hat he had stuffed in his bag. He had found it just lying on the side of the road a couple of hours ago. It was a dark blue baseball cap with an adjustable band, so it fit him perfectly. There was an emblem on the hat with the words 'Red Sox-2018 World Series Champions'. He thought the baseball cap was unique because the lettering on it was a neon red, and glowed in the dark. Then it hit him. Boy, am I stupid, he said to himself. He stopped on the side of the road and began rummaging through his backpack. He found the hat almost at the bottom of his bag. It was in excellent condition and he put it on his head and started walking again.

He once more continued counting his steps and had reached the number of 483. He stopped then because he thought he heard a vehicle coming up from behind him. He turned and looked down the road and sure enough he saw headlights getting closer. He hoisted his bag up on his shoulder more and stuck out his thumb. The vehicle slowed down and he saw that it was an old farm truck. In the bed of the truck was some loose hay, a coil of rope and other miscellaneous farm equipment. The truck was an old one, about a 1976 Ford pickup. It had many rusted out spots on it and the motor seemed to be sputtering quite a bit, but he thought, a ride is a ride. He opened the passenger side door and as it creaked he heard the driver say, "You need a ride? I'm only going to Alton though". The hitch hiker smiled and thought how lucky he was for once. He climbed in the truck and said thanks. The first thing he noticed was the odor, like the smell of mold and cow manure. The driver looked old and smelled like the inside of the cab of the truck. The driver was smoking a cigarette and starting coughing, then spit out his window as he flicked the cigarette out also. The old man gave him the creeps, but he was relieved that he would not have to walk as far now.

"My name is Aaron" the hitcher said ."You live around here ?" The driver just grunted, but then replied "Nice hat." Aaron smiled and told him he had found it. He started to make small talk but soon knew the driver wasn't listening and didn't seem a bit interested. About 15 minutes into the ride he felt a dragging sensation coming from the back end of the truck. Oh great, he thought, it's probably a flat tire. The driver pulled over to the side of the road. He had to really give the driver's side door a heavy push to get it open, which he did and Aaron saw him walk to the back of the truck. He noticed that the old man was limping and grumbling to himself. All of a sudden he was standing right at the passenger's door and was just staring at him. Just seeing him like that made Aaron jump, then he thought about all those old slasher movies he had watched when he was young and felt himself tremble a bit. The old man starting coughing again, then he wiped his mouth on the sleeve of his dirty, dark coat. In a gravelly voice he said, "I'm going to need some help," then turned and limped away towards the back of the truck. Aaron got out and walked over to the old man. As he looked at him he saw that the old man had a crow bar in one hand and a four way tire iron in the other hand, which he was spinning like a baton. Aaron felt something strange about the guy. He seemed to be smiling, but it looked more like a grimace on his face. He also noticed that neither of the tires looked flat. The old man asked him to climb into the truck bed, throw down the coil of rope and find the spare tire, which was probably under all the farm debris. After Aaron climbed into the back of the truck he picked up the coil of rope and looked around for the tire. "Nope, not here'" he said. He did find a hand pump, like something you would use to inflate a bicycle tire. He continued to search under everything, then turned and said, "Sorry, no tire." "Never mind, never mind" the old man grumbled. "Just get out of there." As he lifted one leg over the side of the truck he felt the old man grab him by his leg and then throw him onto the ground. He didn't have time to roll away from the old man as he saw him swing the crow bar at his chest. He actually heard bones cracking as he rolled over and moaned. He was trying to stand up when the old man started beating him on his back with the tire iron. He cried out when he realized he couldn't feel his legs. The blows continued until there were no more sounds from Aaron. The old man started laughing, but it was a cruel sound as he dragged the boy into the woods. He propped him up against a tree and tied him to the tree trunk. One more should do it, he thought, then he smashed Aaron's head with the crow bar. He just stood looking at the body, spit again and limped back toward the truck, but he almost forgot about the folded piece of paper in his pocket. He took it out and tucked it under the rope. He saw the baseball cap on the ground, picked it up and smiled a wicked grin. He put the hat on his head, turned for one last look at Aaron, then threw the tools into the bed of the truck. He climbed slowly back behind the steering wheel, turned the ignition on and drove off. He grumbled again, talking to himself. "Like I said, nice hat." Then he started his drive toward Alton, with the truck sputtering all the way.

NORTON'S TAVERN

Marty Norton had owned the Tavern for many years. After the big fire years ago, most of the towns people thought he would also succumb to the lack of business, but Marty loved the place and kept it open because to him, it was like his second home.

Unlike many of the other businesses and homes on Main Street, the Tavern was set back. A cobblestone walkway led to the front door and the small lawn was always neatly mowed. There was a narrow alleyway that was also laid with cobblestone and led around to the rear of the establishment. Marty owned it outright, and had always been frugal with his money during the years, so he had decided to keep the Tavern open. It was all he had anyway. The usual customers kept him busy enough. It was not uncommon to see people playing pinochle, checkers and even chess on late afternoons, especially on weekends in the Winter months. Bill Simons and Nick Bernstein had come by that afternoon for a couple of hours and a couple of shots of Jack Daniels. Today they were sitting at the bar trying to outdo each other as they told some of their favorite jokes to Marty. The radio was on and set to a Country Music Station, and when an old Patsy Kline song started playing they all just sat and reminisced. Bill and Nick said it was time for them to hit the road. They paid their tab and told Marty they were both going back to their farms, which were on the outskirts of town. They headed out the door giving Marty their own versions of "see you later" and "take care". The place was quiet when Marty again noticed the lone figure in a dark coat sitting at one of the back tables of the Tavern. He liked the fancy baseball cap that the old man had on, but didn't recognize him because the hat was pulled way down over his face. "Hey buddy" he said loudly, "you want another one ?" He had already served him two shots of bourbon and a glass of water. There was no response. Marty just shrugged and got his mop and cleaning supplies out. "Listen" he said, "I'm just going to clean up the bathroom real fast, let me know if you want anything, ok?" There was still no response from the man. Marty turned and headed to the bathroom. He knew it wouldn't take long. He'd probably be back behind the bar in about 15 minutes. When he came back around to the bar, he noticed the old man was gone. Marty grabbed a bar cloth and went to clear that back table. He saw something written on a napkin, but the glass of water had blurred some of the words. He picked it up and saw he was still able to read most of it. It said, "This town is going to die." Marty just shook his head and mumbled 'nut case." He cleared and wiped the table down, then went back behind the bar and started scanning the latest Cabela catalog. Something was bothering him but he couldn't quite remember what. He had thought that the old man did look somewhat familiar, but he couldn't place him. He just sighed and thought whoever said that when you got old it was your Golden Years must have been crazy themselves.

THE MURDER AND THE NUNS

Wayne wanted to make a good impression on his Uncle Carl. It was his first time by himself at the shop. There had been a steady stream of customers most of the afternoon. When the store was empty, he kept busy by wiping down the meat cases and sweeping the tile floor.

He had met quite a few of the regular customers and they all seemed friendly enough. There had been one incident though, but he still thought it had been a bit comical. A woman came in to buy a roast, two pounds of hamburger and a pound of bacon. She had two little girls with her, and they were real cuties. He had always gotten along well with children and had even filled a glass container with lollipops for them. He had explained to Uncle Carl that was his 'signature' butcher move, although he noticed that Uncle Carl didn't seem impressed by it. He prepared the order for the woman, but when he bent over to pick up the pen he had dropped on the floor he let out a huge fart. He waited a few seconds but saw the irritated look on the woman's face, then said, "Sorry about that." The two little girls were giggling hysterically but stopped when their mother gave them a curt look. Wayne gave a lollipop to each little girl and watched them as they headed out the door. "Geez" thought Wayne, "It's just a natural body function," then started laughing himself.

The guy that was having the big barbecue had already picked up his order of baby back ribs. It was later now and he knew it was going to be slow until closing time. Only the order for the two Nuns were left wrapped and labeled in the refrigerator." Geez" he said to himself, "Two Nuns, I'd better not bend down again. Just my luck I'd let another one rip." He was enjoying the quiet of the late afternoon and started humming one of his favorite tunes. He noticed the white wrapping paper on the counter was getting low. He wiped his hands and headed to one of the supply closets in the back room. He checked all the shelves for a role of paper for the dispenser, but couldn't find any. He finally saw a new box that hadn't been opened yet, so he grabbed the box cutter, opened it and took out one of the heavy rolls of wrapping paper. He heard the bell over the door ring as it always did when someone came into the shop. He thought of the Nuns and shouted out, "Be right there." He picked up the roll of paper and as he closed the supply door he heard footsteps. "Is that you, Uncle Carl?" As he turned around he saw a dark figure, and that was the last thing Wayne would ever see as a massive blow to the side of his head caused him to collapse dead on the floor.

The two Nuns, Sister Madeline and Sister Teresa were riding their bicycles down to the butcher shop. Sister Madeline had checked her watch and knew they were running a bit late, but remembered that Carl kept the store open until 7PM on Thursday evenings. They parked their bikes and Sister Teresa was talking about her special marinade she was going to use for the thick pork cutlets. Her mouth was already watering. They had always been good friends besides being Nuns for many years. Both of them were proud of the little school they ran at the small rectory. Even when Reverend Weinberg came to say Mass every two weeks, he would always tell them how impressed he was with the great job they were doing.

When they opened the door, the bell went off as usual. They walked in but didn't see Carl at the counter. Sister Madeline had an odd feeling and Sister Teresa said, "What is that strange odor?" They waited a couple of minutes. Sister Madeline could hear the sound of a machine running in the back of the shop. She walked to the swinging door that separated the two rooms and gasped as she saw a puddle of blood seeping out from under the door. Sister Teresa also saw it and just stared at the other Nun. Sister Madeline slowly opened the door and that's when the screaming started. Sister Teresa kept screaming, blessing herself and fumbled for her prayer beads. Sister Madeline couldn't believe what she was seeing. There were fingers littering the surface of the floor. A foot without any shoe on it was leaning against the small counter that the big meat slicer was set on, and the slicer was still running. She saw two large meat cleavers, one in a second puddle of blood and the other wedged into the back of the body that was lying face down. "Oh my God," she whispered, as she also made the Sign of the Cross. That's when they both ran for the front door, slipping and sliding in the pools of blood. Sister Teresa just made it outside in time before she started retching between screams. Sister Madeline was praying and crying, then she let out a scream so loud the entire area of Main Street probably heard it.

Old man Sydney was out walking his dog, a mini dachshund, when he heard the screams and then saw the Nuns. As he got closer he could see what looked like spattered blood all over Sister Madeline's habit. Marty from the Tavern came out of his bar and shouted, "What's going on ?" Sister Madeline was blubbering away as Sydney shouted to Marty, "Call the Sheriff, call now!' Marty ran back into the bar, grabbed his phone and called the Sheriff's office.

Carl and his friends had opened a window and their third beer. Arnie shushed them for a second and said, "Do you hear that ? Sounds like screams, and coming from near the butcher shop." They quickly looked out the window. "Oh shit " Bernie said, "What's happened now ?" All three threw their beers in the cooler and were out the front door running down the street. They heard the siren and saw Sheriff Lamberts cruiser fly by them. A couple of blocks away there were people also standing outside the diner to see what all the commotion was about.

Carl, Arnie and Benny pushed their way through the small crowd and looked at the Nuns. Both had their heads down and were praying, while crying. Sister Madeline looked up and saw Carl. Her mouth dropped and her eyes widened as she said, "Carl, you're not dead!" Carl could feel it coming as he screamed, "Shit, Crap, Shit." and ran into the butcher shop. He saw the Sheriff and could hear a machine running. She tried to hold him back but he quickly swung the door open to the back room and moaned. "Oh my God, Wayne," He began stuttering as Sheriff Lambert was pulling him away. Arnie and Benny were in the front room but could see the carnage through the open swinging door. "Carl, Carl" as the Sheriff was almost screeching now. "This is a crime scene, you have to get out." He looked at her, then Arnie and Benny pushed him out the front door. There were a number of people on the street and all were trying to find out exactly what had happened. Sheriff Lambert found the note as she was carefully walking around Wayne's body. It was covered with blood, but the words could still be read, "This town is going to die !" She just shook her head as she started to work the scene.

Rumors were flying through the town faster than the birds up above. Jeanne had walked down to the butcher shop, found out what had occurred then immediately called Gerry at the diner. Gerry told Mike, who told Pinky and others at the diner. Gerry had also called Eileen, who called her son Dave right away. Marty at the Tavern had called a few of his friends. Even old man Sydney started to tell all his neighbors. Benny ran into the twins later and told them. Sister Madeline called Reverend Weinberg, who was at the clinic visiting an ill parishioner. He told Doc Horton who then told his wife Jubilee. Doc Horton's wife spread the story all through the clinic. Sheriff Lambert called Willy Grey Wolf and spoke with him. After she explained what happened, she also told him that it was urgent he came to the station the next day. He had been at Mazer's for a few hours replacing the kitchen door. He was grooming one of his horses when Sheriff Lambert called. Everyone in the town now knew what had happened, that's how a small town works. The Sheriff decided she needed a deputy and was going to offer the position to Willy Grey Wolf.

THE BLACK SEDAN

Alex had ridden his bicycle to the post office the next morning. He too had started worrying a lot about the strange clouds and the much needed rain that never came. One day he was lying in a field with Cooper by his side. He stared at the gray clouds. There seemed to be layers in one spot, and long strip like clouds in another spot. He also thought they were not moving. So weird, and today as he looked at them when he was riding his bike they still appeared the same. He had left Cooper at the farm with Mazer. He didn't want her alone since Olsen was gone. She was not the same, and he could still hear her crying at night while he was supposed to be sleeping.

Doc Horton had stopped by for a visit the day after the terrible incident. He had sat with Mazer for quite some time, both of them talking softly. When he was getting ready to leave he asked Alex to walk him to his car. As they walked, Doc Horton told him that Mazer had suffered a trauma, and would not be herself for a while. He also explained that people grieve in their own way and he believed only time would help her. Alex nodded and said he understood. After the Doctor left, Alex vowed that he would keep a close eye on his Aunt Mazer.

On his way home from the post office he decided to stop at the diner. Alex had three quarters in his pocket and he was hoping he could persuade Gerry or Pinky into a piece of pie, especially if they had any chocolate cream. That was his favorite. He parked his bike out front and when he entered the diner he noticed it was quieter than usual. Even when Mike the cook rang the bell at his kitchen station there was a lack of enthusiasm as he said ," Order up." He saw Pinky a few booths down taking an order. He couldn't believe how big her stomach was. To him it looked as though there was a watermelon stuffed down the front of her pants. He had so many questions about pregnancy, but kept them to himself. He had tried to talk to Gerry, skirting around the subject but all she said was, "Now Alex, there are some things little boys should not concern themselves with." She let it go at that. Little did she know he knew a lot more than she suspected.

He sat down at the counter. He had taken his three quarters out of his pocket and stacked them next to one of the napkin dispensers. He saw Gerry come from the back kitchen carrying a tray of freshly made pies, just in time before the lunch crowd. Gerry saw him and said, "Hey, little man, how are you ? How is Mazer? I'm planning on taking a ride out there tomorrow, so please tell her, Ok? I hope she's doing better." She eyed the three quarters on the counter and smiled. After a few minutes she carried a small plate with a piece of his favorite pie and put it on the counter in front of him. He smiled from ear to ear and said, "Gee thanks Gerry. Then he pushed the three quarters toward her. " Put that away" she said," Your money's no good here." He blushed and grabbed a fork and started digging into his pie. Mike the cook had been watching him. What a great kid he thought. Mazer had sure done a terrific job of raising those two boys. With that thought he shouted over to Alex. "Hey kid, how is Eli doing ? Have you heard from him lately?" Alex nodded as he swallowed a mouthful of pie. He washed it down with a gulp of milk. He looked at Mike and told him they had received two letters about two and a half weeks ago. "I just came from the post office and sent out three more letters to him today." "Great" Mike responded. "Next time you write him please tell him I said howdy and we all sure do miss him, Ok?" "You've got it Mike," said Alex. All of a sudden he felt Pinky beside him and he knew what was coming next. Sure enough, she gave him one of her special kisses on his cheek and smiled at him. He was trying not to stare at her stomach and she knew it. She leaned down on her elbow, looking straight at him and said, "It's okay to look Alex," after all I am pregnant" and started to laugh.

Not too many people were talking about the horrible event at the butcher shop. It was closed of course, and Carl was now mourning for his cousin Wayne. He had come to the diner very early in the morning and just sat and ate a small breakfast. Mike the cook wanted to talk to him, but Gerry had just shook her head with a firm no intended. She later whispered to Mike, "Just leave him alone for now. I also do not want anyone telling Mazer yet, she is carrying enough heartache. Do you understand?" Mike and some of the others all nodded and went back to their daily chores. The lunch crowd was starting. Booths were filling up and all the employees were getting into a quick serve mode. The energy in the diner had changed quickly, even Alex could sense it. He had finished his pie and small glass of milk, wiped his mouth with his napkin and shouted, "Thanks guys." The noise from the diner verified lunch was on.

Alex went outside and was checking one of the tires on his bike. He thought it looked low, but would ride slowly back to the farm just in case. Then it happened so fast that Alex just stood, stunned and confused. Suddenly everything changed and things seemed to happen in slow motion. He saw Gerry and Pinky and a few of the customers staring out the windows of the diner. He also saw that Eileen had pulled up and was just leaning on her vehicle. The official military sedan with two Marines in class A uniforms were driving by. Gerry and Eileen knew immediately who they were and why they were here in town. They were on their way to the farm. One of the men in the car was a Chaplin, the other Marine's task was for the duty of death notification. Mike stopped cooking and wiped his eyes. He knew when Mazer saw that government vehicle, the black sedan out in front of the house, she would know. The words would not even have to be spoken at first, and the grief would already be starting. There was a crash of plates and Pinky fainted but not before one of the truckers caught her before she almost fell to the floor. Another customer helped lay her across one of the front booths. Gerry shouted at Mike "Call Doc Horton right now." He didn't need to be told twice and was already on the phone. Eileen had stuck her head in the front door and said, "Gerry, I'm going to Mazers. I'll take Alex with me, I'm just going to put his bike in the back of the Rover." Gerry nodded, feeling tears streaming down her face. "I have to stay here with Pinky, she's due anytime and Mike called Doc Horton. I'm sure he'll be here right away." Eileen quickly put Alex in the Rover, then threw his bike in the back and took off for the farm. Alex just sat and stared, not saying a word. As Eileen was driving, she wondered just how much more her good friends could bare. A word was not spoken as they drove to the farm.

The farm was very quiet that day. Mazer had been feverishly working in her garden, pulling weeds and talking. She had been praying that morning. She looked up and asked the Divine Creator, her (Magic Guy in the Sky) for strength and courage. Many times she glanced at Olsen's grave and felt such heartache. Even Buttercup and Hannah were quiet, just standing up against the paddock fence, watching Mazer.

She heard a car pull up out front, and walked into the house through the kitchen to the front door. When she saw the two men get out of the Military Sedan she knew, and just fell to her knees. They saw her through the screen door and quickly walked in and knelt beside her. The Chaplain said they were here to speak with Amanda Greenstone. For a few seconds the name did not register with her. Then, almost in a whisper she said "Yes, that is me but everyone calls me Mazer." For the second time in just a few days she actually felt outside herself as the two Marines led her to the sofa, then sat on either side of her. She knew they were talking but refused to hear them. She kept saying, "This cannot be true, I cannot believe it." They were silent for a minute, then the second Marine was talking and the Official Notification was spoken. Just then Eileen came flying through the door with Alex behind her. She ran to

Mazer and embraced her. They both starting crying. Mazer was moaning and rocking back and forth, saying, "No, no, not my Eli. Please God, no. This cannot be happening." Alex just stood next to the door and was sobbing quietly. Cooper had run next to him and whined, just staring at Alex. The two Marines left about an hour later. Their condolences and heartfelt words still filled the room.

THE BIG MISTAKE

Little did anyone know that Eli had hitched a ride after arriving at Camp Pendleton. He had tried over and over to call Mazer, but her phone was still out of order for some reason. He had fortunately been able to find a transport plane that was flying to Fort Leonard Wood, a small Marine Corp base in Missouri. It was mainly used for training and education and was located near ST. Roberts Town. From there he would try to catch any means of transportation to Alton, even if he had to hitchhike the rest of the way. He felt an urgency inside him but didn't know why. He had about five hours left before he would reach Missouri. He tried to sleep but found it almost impossible, and just kept staring at the photo of the sonogram the entire flight home.

After a while, he noticed a look of grave concern on the Marine Lieutenant who was also on his way to Missouri. He was talking on a satellite phone and turned his back from Eli. Eli could hear dribs and drabs of the conversation. "Yes Sir," said the Lt., I totally understand, but how could something like this happen? Yes, yes Colonel." Then he was interrupted on the other end of the phone. Whoever he was talking to sounded a bit brash, but the Lt. was listening intently. The conversation went on for another five minutes, then the Lt. ended the call saying, "I do so understand and I will handle it personally right away Sir. Yes Colonel, he is sitting a few feet from me now. Yes, I will call you back as soon as I speak with Cpl. Rosker." That is when Eli's ears pricked up. The Lt. shut down the satellite phone. He took a deep breath and sat down next to Eli. After he sat down he said, " I have some disturbing news for you. I just want you to listen to me and no questions until I finish, do you understand Cpl. ?" "Yes Sir" Eli replied, and he suddenly imagined all kinds of bad news might be coming. The Lt. started off by emphasizing that a serious error had been made back at Camp Leatherneck. Somehow, a new Medic had incorrectly identified the wrong causality as he prepared the body of another Marine. He explained that Eli's dog tags had been found and he had mistakenly been listed as KIA, killed in action. Eli just sat there. The Lt. continued and just shook his head. He then told him that two Marines, according to procedure , had traveled to his Aunt's home and carried out their duty of the Notification of Death. I am so sorry for this grave error and the military has been desperately trying to notify the team that were there. They just did that a while ago. One is a Chaplain and he is beside himself. The both of them are now heading back to your family to correct this terrible mistake. We have not been able to contact your Aunt by telephone. "Is there anyone else we can call at this time?" Eli was dumbfounded, and thought for a few seconds. My fiancé Pinky he said, but then the Lt. interrupted him saying they already attempted several calls to a J. Pinkton, but there was no answer there either. Eli's mind was racing. He stood and started pacing. He turned toward the Lt. and now was showing clear anger. "How could this happen? Imagine my poor family and friends. They think I'm dead. My fiancé is due to have our baby any day now. All I want to do is get home as fast as I can." The Lt. stood and talked to him again. "Soldier, I know " and again said, "This has been a disastrous mistake, but it will be rectified, I promise you that." He grabbed the satellite phone before he walked to the front of the plane, then said, "Give me a list of any phone numbers you think would be helpful. I will personally call all of them myself. I promise you and again I am sorry." Eli quickly wrote on a notepad that the LT. had handed him and gave it back to the Lt. right away. He looked at the LT and said, "I have a favor to ask, please come back and give me any updates, ok Sir ?" The Lt. nodded, then both saluted. Once again Eli sat and became lost in his thoughts. He felt sick to his stomach, held his head down and just murmured, "Okay Pinky, Aunt Mazer and Alex, I will be home soon." He checked his watch and knew time would not go by fast enough. He couldn't believe that this had happened, or even that it could happen. He continued to sit quietly and started to pray. He sure hoped someone was listening to him.

THE APPEARANCE OF CHARLOTTE PEARL

While Mike was trying to get in touch with Doc Horton, Gerry grabbed a clean towel, soaked it in cold water and put it on Pinky's forehead. She was so nervous, especially with so many people standing around. She felt like she would faint herself. She glanced outside for a second and saw Jeanne heading for the diner. Gerry ran outside and just about dragged her in, all the while telling her what had happened. She felt such a relief that Jeanne was there now. Jeanne had been a registered nurse for 30 years in a big city hospital until she retired. She had returned to Alton to care for her elderly parents, who had both passed on a few years ago. As soon as Jeanne saw Pinky laying in the booth, she took over. She took her pulse, checked her pupils and started to lightly tap Pinky's face. A few minutes later she heard a soft moan come from Pinky. "I think she's coming around" someone said. Gerry looked over at Jeanne and saw a look of concern on her face and knew something wasn't right. Pinky's stomach was hard and the moans coming from her were not from the fainting episode. Jeanne looked at Gerry and said, "I think she's in labor." Just then Mike hollered over to them and said, "I got Doc Horton on the phone!" Jeanne ran over and grabbed the phone and started talking, then listening to the Dr. "Ok, sure, ok" she said. She hung up the phone, looked at everyone and said, "We have to get Pinky to the clinic immediately, and I mean now." One of the customers came forward and said, "I've got a station wagon, we can lay her down in the back and there's plenty of room for you gals also." Gerry and Jeanne both started giving orders. "We need a blanket and a pillow," Jeanne said. Gerry told Mike to close the diner early. Two of the bigger guys picked Pinky up from under her arms. Her moans were getting louder and more frequent. As they were almost at the station wagon, her water broke. "Oh shit," one of the guys said. Then one of the customers, a huge trucker, appeared and just swept Pinky up in his arms and laid her across the back seat of the station wagon. Jeanne and Gerry jumped in the front seat. Gerry looked at the man and asked him his name. "Everyone calls me Buster," he said. "I never knew that," Gerry replied. Buster looked at her and told her "Yeah right, I've only been coming to your diner for three years now." He turned the key, but there was no sound. He tried again and it was the same. He began mumbling, "Damn piece of crap, I've been meaning to sell it but never got around to it." He opened the driver's side door and saw that the girls were starting to panic. They both stopped when he gave them a look and said, "Don't say a word." He grabbed something from the floor behind the seat, then got out and opened the hood. He started banging away at something. He shouted, "That should do it, try to start it now." Gerry slid over behind the steering wheel, turned the key and it started right up. Buster slammed the hood down and got behind the wheel again. They made it to the clinic in ten minutes.

Doc Horton, one of the nurses and an orderly ran out with a stretcher. Pinky was awake now and as they got her on the stretcher she started holding her stomach and screaming. "Oh boy," Gerry said and started looking anxious. Less than two hours later Charlotte Pearl

Pinkton came into the world. She was like a pink princess, with wide green eyes, a heart shaped mouth and a tuft of blonde hair. Pinky was just fine, but started crying as she held her new daughter.

Three hours later the doctor checked on both of them. He was astonished that the birth had gone so well but was concerned about Pinky's state of mind. The nurses had already walked her to the bathroom, and she kept telling them she was okay, just a little tired. She didn't tell them that she was determined to go home with her new baby the next day. She had to try to find out any information about Eli, and what had happened. Little did she know that a few hours away Eli was alive and well, but was having some bad luck of his own. The transport plane he was on started to have some engine problems and had to make an emergency landing at a small private airport in the Dakota's. Everyone walked off the plane quickly and were then ushered into the small terminal. Eli was beside himself. The Lt. still had not been able to contact anyone in Alton. The Lt. had also decided not to inform Eli yet that the original two notification Marines had been involved in a minor automobile accident while they were on their way back to Eli's aunt's home. He knew that Eli was stressed enough at this time. He had told Eli he called a Jeanne Boise, the local butcher shop, an Eileen Arel and Gerry's Diner. No one answered at any of these numbers. He even tried the Aunt again, but there was only a busy signal. Eli thought about Sheriff Lambert, called the number himself but was just connected with the answering machine. He did leave a lengthy message though. Unfortunately Sheriff Lambert was with Carl, trying to console him and also writing a detailed report for the county coroner.

Eli had waited almost three hours with still no word on any departure yet. He was irritable, tired and out of patience. He glared at one of the pilots and shouted, "I have to get home, do you understand that !" Neither one of them said a word while Eli went outside and made his way to one of the other hangars. He was going to find a way home no matter what.

Meanwhile, back in Alton, Eileen was watching the front door when the local telephone repair team came. Finally, she said to herself. The two man crew greeted her but saw she was not in a good mood, so they went right to work, not saying a word.

Mazer and Alex were sitting on the sofa and had not moved for an hour. Some papers rustled in Mazers hands now and then. They had been given to her by the Chaplin and the Notification Officer. There was several helpful phone numbers on them the Chaplin said, but Mazer had never looked at them. In about an hour the telephone wires had been fixed and she now had a brand new working phone. Eileen first called her son Dave at the Gas N Go. He picked up on the second ring and excitedly told her that Pinky had had her baby, a perfect little girl, 6 lbs. 8 oz. and both were doing fine. At last, some good news she thought. She asked some questions about the station and he said everything was okay. He asked if he could close up a little earlier that evening. He was going to ride out to Tom Choate's farm and help him fix his John Deere tractor. She said that was fine but she told him to take the extra cell phone with him and keep it on at all times. He said okay and she reminded him it was in the top drawer of her desk in her office. He promised he would do that, then also mentioned that there had been two more break-ins in the town. Someone had managed to steal a few things at Benny's hardware store this time. A pair of good boots, some small tools, a large hunting knife and a black rain parka were missing. "Things are really getting kind of weird, Mom," he said. She agreed and thought to herself, when is this going to stop? She told him she would be in touch later and ordered him in a mother's way to make sure he wore his helmet when he rode that damn motorcycle out to Tom Choates farm. He just said, "Oh Mom, you know I'll be careful, love you and talk to you later." She hung up and told Mazer and Alex that Pinky had had the baby. She gave her all the details and the good news seemed to lift their spirits. Mazer noticed that Eileen looked very tired, so she suggested to her that she should go home. They would be fine. Eileen was not totally convinced, but finally gave in. She had decided she'd take a shower, change her clothes and head to the clinic to visit Pinky and the baby. She was driving home about twenty minutes later.

Willy Grey Wolf knocked on the front door and walked in. Mazer came out of the kitchen and smiled. He had a new crisp light blue shirt on with dark blue slacks. A well-worn leather belt was around his waist, holding a vintage leather holster that carried a Glock 9mm pistol. On his shirt was a shiny badge with the words 'Deputy, Town of Alton'. "You look so handsome" said Mazer "you really do. "Nah, I feel like a geek." No, no you look so, hmm, official." Mazer replied. "Would you like some coffee, and I made lemon squares, please come in." He asked about Alex and she told him he took Cooper for a walk. They talked about Pinky and the new baby, about the break ins that had happened in the town again and she asked about Carl. He saw the papers that the Chaplain and Notification Officer had left for her. She just looked at him and said "I just don't believe it, I really can't. There's something wrong, I can feel it. What's that old saying, like you have an itch in your craw. Something is just not right." Willy just sat there, finishing his lemon square and coffee. He knew that loved ones many times just refused to believe such news, but he also knew Mazer was very intuitive and wondered if she just might be on to something. He was going back to the Sheriff's office later to check any messages and make some calls of his own. Before he could even ask, she placed the papers on the table in front of him. "Willy? You call please. You call and find out what really happened to my Eli, ok?" He nodded, stood up from the table and they hugged, and she started crying again. "I had this dream of the Tree of Stories, I also had a dream of a big storm, then I dreamt of Jacob. Something is just not right." she said again. Then she felt the loneliness and the quiet as she watched Willy walk out to his truck.

Part Six

CHESTER HENLEY

Mazer would never have imagined that a few hundred miles away, Eli had finally come into a bit of luck. He had been walking through the few hangers at the small airport, when he met a man named Chester Henley. Chester was staring at one of the vending machines, trying to decide between chips or cupcakes. He heard someone behind him, turned and saw a young Marine. He shook the Marines hand and said, "You want something to eat?" Eli shook his head and said, "No thanks, but I appreciate the offer." Chester Henley was an older man with a full head of the reddest hair he had ever seen, and a mustache to match. He wore gold rimmed spectacles, jeans and a polo shirt, but Eli couldn't help but notice the exquisite Bombers Jacket he also had on. Chester saw him staring at his jacket, which had many Military patches on it. He smiled at Eli and said, "I was a pilot in the first Desert Storm war. Flying's in my blood." He bought chips and cupcakes and also two bottles of Pepsi from the soda machine. He handed a Pepsi to Eli and said, "Come on, every Marine has a story and I sure would like to hear yours.

They sat down on a nearby wooden bench and after Eli finished telling him everything that had happened, Chester just shook his head..

“That’s quite a story,” he said. He looked over at the Twin Engine Cessna 340. “That’s my plane. Had a problem with one of the back lights and that’s why I’m waiting around here. It should be all set in an hour.” He looked at Eli and said, “Tell you what son, I’d be more than happy to have some company when I fly out of here. I’m heading to Springfield Branson National Airport in lower Missouri. My family is going to meet me there. I have a great wife and three daughters. Imagine, three girls, their ages ranging from 8 years to 14 years and they’re all gorgeous with red hair and freckles. Eli could hear the pride in his voice and he even took a picture out of his wallet to show him. Eli looked at it and thought of Pinky and his new daughter on the way. He told Chester “You have a beautiful family. I’m so happy for you.” Chester smiled as he put the photo back in his wallet. “You know Eli, when you have children, it changes your entire perspective on life, it really does. I just worry about one thing,” “What’s that?” Eli said. Chester started laughing and said, “I worry about how I’m going to pay for three weddings.” Then they both were laughing as Eli and Chester stood up. He patted Eli on the back and said, “Come on, let’s go see how soon my plane will be ready. We have to get you home .” Eli beamed, as they both walked over to Chester’s Twin Engine Cessna. He knew he still had a ways to go before he got home to Pinky.

The first thing Eli noticed while sitting in the co-pilots seat of Chester’s Cessna was the stars. There was not a cloud in the dark sky, just millions of twinkling lights above and around them. They hadn’t talked much for a while because Chester was frequently checking all the instruments and responding to the radio chatter now and then. Chester told him that they would be descending soon, and Eli saw the lights of small towns and also the airport tower coming closer. He felt his heart pounding and fidgeted in his seat. Chester noticed this and told him to relax, they would be landing in about 20 minutes. As the time passed so many thoughts crowded his mind. He knew he was still a few hours away from Alton, but would tackle that problem after they landed. All he could think about was Pinky and getting home. He could feel the plane descending and heard Chester verifying coordinates with the control tower. He saw Chester press the landing gear instrument and braced himself. A few minutes later he felt a small bounce and knew the plane was now on the landing strip and slowly traveling down one of the runways. A man with positioning lights stood on the runway and Chester easily turned the Cessna toward the small hanger at the airport. Even though the engines were still running, he knew the plane was stopped. Chester slapped him on the knee, smiled and said, "See, nothing to it, we made it safe and sound." The noise of the engines ceased and Chester started shutting all the cockpit's lights down. Eli followed him as he walked to the side door of the plane. He heard a hiss and saw the plane's stairway open. They both grabbed all their gear and walked out onto the tarmac and into the large terminal. All of a sudden Eli heard shrieks and cheers as three red headed , freckled young girls ran toward their dad, Chester. He had a big smile on his face and was almost knocked over when his entire family jumped up to hug him. His wife gave him a big kiss and started calming down the girls. "Wait, wait" Chester said, "I want you to meet someone." As he introduced Eli, he told them all a short version of his story, then looked at his wife. Sharon, his wife, went over to Eli, gave him a hug then said, "I guess we better help you on your way." Their SUV was parked near and she looked at her husband and said, "You know we have plenty of room. We can give him a ride to that big truck stop two exits away. We would gladly bring you all the way, but we're expected at a special family reunion in about an hour. Unfortunately, we can't miss it." Eli said that would be just great and thanked them all, saying they had done far too much as it was. About 40 minutes later, they dropped him off at the exit where the truck stop was. He stood waving at Chester and his family as they drove away. He picked up his duffel bag and started his walk to the truck stop.

BONES

The small cabin had been built in 1954 by Jeremy's dad and was located in the easterly part of the forest. It had weathered well, as they say, and as Jeremy stood on the front porch only good memories came easily to him. It was his 29th birthday. He has decided to take a short sabbatical from teaching at the state university about 100 miles away from Alton. His first stop in the town was at Arel's Gas-n-Go. He filled the jeep, bought a few basics for the cabin and smiled as he saw his favorite treat, Twinkies, in the bag also. Eileen gave him a big hug as he shook his head because it had been years and she still remembered how he loved Twinkies. She told him how impressed she was that the boys in the back of the jeep were so well behaved. "You can thank Willy Grey Wolf for that" Jeremy said. He and Willy had been friends for years and without his help, the boys, two chocolate brown Labrador Retrievers named Dakota and Phoenix, would never have been trained well enough for their first hunting trip. His next stop was the Diner. He ordered some food to go but not before Gerry and Mike the cook made him sit and enjoy a fresh cup of coffee and a piece of pie. Mike sat next to him and regaled of all the latest news about Alton. "Seems like a lot has happened since I left, and what's with those darn strange clouds ? I have never seen anything like it before." Mike packed his order up for him, leaned over and quietly said "Believe me, between you and me, no one ever has." As Jeremy drove away down Main Street, he noticed how quiet the town was, almost too quiet. He started thinking about the hunting trip. The gear was packed and the 28 Gauge shotgun was cleaned and tested. He pulled up to the cabin and felt such a sense of solace and knew he has made the right decision. He was going to enjoy this quiet time at the cabin with his boys.

At 6:30 AM the next morning, he was up making coffee and let the boys out. He filled his thermos, grabbed his hunting pack, gun and two bottles of water for the dogs then started walking down the main logging trail. He was hoping the dogs would work off some of their energy before they reached the outskirts of the duck pond. As they walked he realized how the great fire has changed the forest in so many ways, but his father has taught him well on all their hunting trips and he felt confident he was heading the right way. He stopped and sat on an old fallen log, poured himself a coffee and ate two packs of Twinkies as he watched the dogs do their "circle and sniff" routine. He checked his watch, closed his eyes and leaned back against another tree for a minute and actually fell asleep. All of a sudden his eyes snapped open and he woke with a start, immediately becoming aware of the quiet and stillness of the forest. The dogs, where were the dogs? He felt a panic and his heart start racing. He called the dogs over and over, then started a quick run down the main trail. About 20 minutes later he felt a sense of relief when he heard a dog barking,, saw a small trail to the left and headed that way. Phoenix was actually running toward him with what looked light a large stick. The dog dropped it at Jeremy's feet and that's when he saw it was a long bone. He didn't have to say a word to the brown Lab when he turned and ran, with Jeremy right behind him. He knew he was leading him to the other dog, Dakota. They found Dakota digging in a hole near an old oak tree. Evidently he had been pretty busy as he kept pulling bones from the hole and piling them together. Jeremy thought it was probably the carcass of a deer that had been dead for quite some time, but then Dakota pulled a human skull from the site and dropped it at Jeremys feet. He leashed both dogs and felt himself shaken, then pulled out his cell phone. He saw he had only one bar left on it but called 911 right away. He crossed his fingers and after the third ring knew it was Willy Grey Wolf. "Willy, Willy, this is Jeremy Judd, I need your help right away." Willy tried to calm him down and asked him where he was. Jeremy told him his story then also noticed the phone was breaking up. "Not sure Willy, I'm near a large old oak tree, have the dogs with me but don't know how far from the main logging road I am. Then there was silence on the phone for a few seconds, but he could still hear Willy faintly. His last words were "Jeremy, use the dogs and the colors" then the phone went dead. Jeremy had been taught well by his father in his hunting skills and knew what Willy meant by "colors". He took two cans of red spray paint from his pack and marked the old oak tree with a red circle and continued to do so with all the larger trees as he and the dogs headed back to the cabin. He now knew that there would be a visible trail to the pile of bones. He was relieved to see Willy Grey Wolf pull up to the cabin. He put the dogs inside then he and Willy followed the red circles to the gravesite. It was getting late but Jeremy watched as Willy carefully removed more bones and also found pieces of tattered material. Suddenly his friends hands trembled as he pulled up what resembled a running shoe. Willy dusted it off and looked inside and saw a name printed on the inside nylon flap-it said-Jane Golden. He carefully placed it on top of the pile of bones and told Jeremy that this was a crime scene now. They both wrapped a roll of police tape around a ten foot area of the trees and headed back to the barn, with nothing but silence between them. At the cabin Willy called Sheriff Lambert and told her everything and as she listened her voice quivered when she told him she would make the necessary calls to the State Coroner, the Forensic Team and the State Police. She would also have to make the hardest call of all to Sydney Golden, Janes grandfather. He had never given up hope in finding Jane, but at least now he would learn the truth and perhaps a form of closure would finally help his broken heart.

ALEX AND COOPER

Alex had told Aunt Mazer that he was taking Cooper for a walk, but he didn't tell her where he was headed. For some reason he was drawn to the Great house and started walking that way. It was almost an hour away on foot, plus Cooper kept exploring the woods on the side of the gravel road which led to the Great house. As Alex got closer he thought the house looked scary. All the lower windows and doors had been boarded up, which gave it an ominous look. The shingles were faded, and the yard around the house was covered with high weeds and even a few wildflowers had grown here and there. An old cement birdbath was crumbling and he also saw that a large Maple tree had fallen down on one side of the house. He started to walk all around the area of the house. Cooper was doing his own version of investigation, trotting behind Alex with his nose to the ground. When Alex came to the back of the house, he saw the bulkhead that led to the utility part of the basement. He had remembered that his Uncle Jacob had lived in the main part of the basement that was an apartment, but that was securely boarded up. The metal bulkhead doors were rusted, along with the handles. There were even some large dents in the doors themselves. Through the handles of the doors was a thick chain that had a large padlock attached to both ends. Boy, he thought to himself, Uncle Willy and his friends sure did a thorough job of closing up the house. Cooper was running around and had already chased a squirrel. He was feeling like he really had accomplished something. He ran to the back of the house where Alex was and sniffed around the bulkhead and started whining. He even started to dig on one side of the metal structure, then barked a few times. Alex just looked at the dog and said, "I do not want to play stick now boy." Cooper barked again trying to get his attention. Alex picked up a long stick and started to jiggle the old chain. That's when he noticed it. The chain was old and rusty, but the padlock on it seemed shiny and somewhat new. He also saw it wasn't clasped. He felt a chill, looked at Cooper then pulled the chain through the metal handles. The chain fell to the ground and the padlock bounced near his feet. He went over to the doors and tried lifting them. He was surprised when they swung open without much effort on his part. He looked down the basement stairs and saw nothing but a black abyss. He kept looking down into the basement and wished he had a flashlight. He slowly walked down the steps with Cooper right behind him. It took a while for his eyes to adjust to the dark, but he did notice one small basement window that had a sliver of light coming through it. He had kept the big stick with him and was walking around the basement like a blind person, using the stick to maneuver around some old boxes, broken jars and a bunch of old pipes that were scattered all over the floor. All of a sudden Cooper started barking, and it wasn't his 'play' bark. Alex tried to see what was in the corner that Cooper was concentrating on. It looked like a dark lurking figure. He held his breath, then finally realized what it was, called the dog, and told him it was only the old large furnace. He was pretty sure the tube like figure near it was a water heater. Cooper still didn't like it and gave out a couple of low growls as he made his way over to Alex. Alex carefully walked over to the small basement window. He saw there was only a piece of rotted canvas covering it. He reached up with his stick and wiped off most of the cob webs and then easily tore off the canvas cover. It was just a small thick glassed window, but at least there was a good bit of light for him to be able to scan the rest of the basement. He turned and looked around while Cooper was sniffing all over the basement floor. He didn't see anything of real interest. There was an old sewing machine, some milk crates, a few broken garden tools and an old tricycle. I bet that had been Eli's he thought. Cooper was sniffing at some mouse droppings and then found an old small tool handle, which he excitedly brought over to Alex and dropped it at his feet. Alex looked at it, shook his head and said, "Not now boy, we'll play stick later I promise." Something had caught Alex's full attention. There was a set of stairs leading up to the main part of the house. He didn't think twice as he walked over to the stairway, told Cooper to stay, and started slowly walking up the stairs. There were about ten steps that lead to the door into the house. He ran up the stairs after the first two steps and stared at the door. There was a brass doorknob, he reached out and tried to turn it, but found it was locked. He then tried pushing the door while turning the knob but it wouldn't budge. The door was a heavy hardwood and seemed really solid. He looked down at Cooper, shrugged and said, "Oh well, we tried, right fella?" All of a sudden he froze. He could hear footsteps up above him. He was going to shout, "Hello" but decided against it when he heard a low guttural growl from Cooper. Alex used the railing and took two steps at a time coming back down the stairs. Now he could even hear the upstairs floor creaking and a pounding sound. He looked at Cooper and ran as fast as he could out of the basement through the bulkhead. He didn't stop to close the doors or put the chain back on, but he did pick up the padlock and kept running down the dusty road with Cooper right behind him.

About fifteen minutes later, feeling his heart pounding, he stopped for a minute. He could still see part of the small windows at the top of the house. He started running again after he thought he saw a face staring back at him. He made it home in record time.

When he got to the farm he and Cooper were covered in dust from the dry, gravel road. He was trying to catch his breath before he saw Aunt Mazer. He put the padlock in his pants pocket and went in the house. Aunt Mazer was hanging clothes outside when she heard Alex and Cooper. "I'm home" then he ran to his room. "About time " she said, “I was getting concerned. I guess you and Cooper had a good walk.” She barely heard him reply, “Sure did” as he hid the padlock in his sock drawer. He plopped down on his bed with Cooper beside him and thought about his next move.

PINKY GOES HOME

It was 5:30 A,M. She was awake, had changed her clothes Jeanne had brought her from her house and was pacing back and forth. Every few minutes Pinky would walk to the door of her small room at the clinic and glance towards the main desk. She was hoping to catch Doc Horton early and coax him into releasing her and the baby that morning. Her mind was spinning. She had just changed Charlotte's diaper and fed her. She placed her back into the small bassinet and the baby fell asleep right away. Even Jeanne had commented on what a good baby she was.

About 6:30 A.M. She heard footsteps heading toward her room. The door opened and Eileen quietly entered. They both hugged then Eileen started telling her how she snuck in early through a side door they never locked. Eileen looked at the baby, then at Pinky and said, "Can I?" "Of course you can" replied Pinky and Eileen picked up the little pink bundle. Both of the women were teary eyed as Eileen walked around the room with the baby in her arms. "I want to go home today," said Pinky. Eileen just looked at her and tried to convince her that having another day of quiet and rest would be good for her, especially considering all she'd been through. Pinky just shook her head, glanced out the door again and said, "No, I want to go home. I have to be home and that's final. No buts about it." "Well," Eileen said, "I can certainly understand that, especially since all that's been happening and now knowing Eli is on his way home. God bless him, you must be so happy." She was walking around the room humming to the baby that was still in her arms when she noticed Pinky was just staring at her, her face as white as a sheet. Eileen laid the baby down in her bassinet and stood in front of Pinky. "Jenn " she said, "Pinky, what is wrong ?" Once again tears were running down Pinky's face, but this time she was smiling. "Eileen, I thought Eli had been killed?" " Oh my God, Oh my God, I am so sorry. I thought you knew." said Eileen. "You didn't hear?" She sat Pinky down on the bed and thought to herself, I really opened my big mouth this time. "No one told me anything, tell me, I want to know everything that's been going on in the town." Eileen sighed and sat next to her, thinking where do I start. She talked and talked nonstop. Pinky just nodded occasionally. She told her about Willy Grey Wolf being deputized, how Benny's store was broken into and just last night an old truck of Tom Choates had been stolen. She was very explicit about Willy getting a message from Eli on the Sheriff's machine, but no one knew where he was. Pinky was smiling and said, "I do, he's on his way home. He's coming home to me and Charlotte." The energy in the room changed and Pinky had become ecstatic, laughing and crying at the same time.

At that moment Doc Horton and one of the nurses entered the room. Pinky's tone was very firm when she told the Doctor "I'm going home today. I have to be there when Eli gets back. I don't want any arguments about this, I am going home! Doc Horton looked at her and knew it would be futile to talk her into staying one more day. He looked at the nurse and told her to get all the necessary paperwork ready. He did a quick but thorough exam on both Pinky and the baby. Pinky was talking a mile a minute and could hardly contain herself.

Jeanne was walking into the clinic toward Pinky's room and heard all the commotion. She ran in and Eileen grabbed her arm and said "She didn't know. She had no idea Eli is on his way home. The Doctor is discharging her today, it's unbelievable." Jeanne did not like the idea of Pinky being home alone with the new baby. She insisted on staying at Pinky's house with her and the baby, at least until Eli arrived. Pinky was more than grateful, and her hand shook as she signed 'Jenn P. Pinkton' and 'Eli Rosker' on the birth certificate.

Eileen got up off the bed where she had been sitting. She seemed pensive but then said, "I have to call Mazer, she probably doesn't know either. Her phone is working again, but I don't know if Willy knew that. He probably hasn't called her yet. I'm going to the diner." She hugged Pinky and Jeanne and said, "I'm out of here. There's so much to do."

Eileen actually ran into the diner. Gerry had a full platter in her hands, almost dropped it but set it on the counter. "Now what? What's the matter?" She didn't think she could handle any more bad news but just waited for Eileen to talk. Eileen spoke loudly hoping that all the customers in the diner would hear her also. The place went silent, no pots and pans clanging, no bell ringing, and no sound of plates and cups being stacked, getting ready for the dishwasher. Just so many faces staring at her waiting. Mike the cook had come out from the kitchen, looked around then said to Eileen "Speak woman, what is it ?" Eileen told everyone the news. Gerry gasped and covered her mouth and Mike the cook actually did a 'happy dance', There were shouts and cheers and smiles. Eileen just plopped down in a booth, looked at Gerry and asked, "Could I please have a big cup of coffee?" Gerry with tears in her eyes told Eileen "You can have anything you want."

Mazer had just finished the few dishes she had in the sink. She had also washed and dried the small ceramic bowl that was decorated with cat prints and had Olsen's name on it. She didn't want to cry anymore, but felt such gloom as she put the cat bowl away on the top shelf of the cabinet. Alex was out mowing the lawn. She thought she would go out to the garden and pick vegetables. She was looking for her garden basket when the phone rang. She put her garden gloves and straw hat down on the back of the sofa and picked up the phone. "Hi Eileen" she said "How are you?"(she had one of those fancy phones now that showed who was calling). She just stood there, almost stoic, and listened intently to her good friend on the other end of the line. Alex noisily came through the front door while trying to take the big stick Cooper was carrying away from him. He succeeded, but then Cooper actually jumped 4 feet in the air and grabbed it back. "No, No Cooper, stop it." Alex once again was trying to take the stick from Cooper's mouth. "Shush, shush" Mazer said loudly, then continued to listen on the phone. After about two to three minutes she slowly hung up the phone, then looked at Alex and almost in a loud whisper said, "Eli's not dead, he's on his way home!"

Everyone in the small town was talking. Any and all news was quickly being spread around to all who would listen. The twins at the What Not Curiosity Shop had prepared a large gift basket. In it were all baby things, little onesies, bibs, two boxes of diapers, booties, bottles and formula, baby powder and shampoo. They also had a warm knitted hat and a thick baby blanket, like a bunting outfit. They had artfully arranged it in a portable baby bathtub. Of course just about everything in it was pink. They carried it over to Pinky's house where Jeanne was vacuuming and dusting quickly. She told them Pinky would love the gift, then the two sisters also started helping getting the house ready. Jeanne was going back to the clinic soon to pick up Pinky and the baby. They should be back about 10:30, she told them. One of the girls cleaned Charlies cage and gave him fresh food and water. Eileen had already stopped by and stuffed the refrigerator with any necessities and even a few goodies.

Sheriff Lambert had been on the phone with Willy Grey Wolf. Carl was still at his new home, not saying much. Willy had been checking in at the butcher shop . The crime scene unit had finally left and he locked up the shop . Carl said he couldn't go in the shop yet and just sat. Sheriff Lambert told him all the good news about Eli and Pinky, and their new baby girl. He nodded and said, "That's a good thing." Benny told the Sheriff that he knew a professional cleaning company one town over. He had called them and he told the Sheriff they would be there late that afternoon to completely wash and sanitize the butcher shop. It would be one less thing for Carl to worry about.

Everyone in town was still grumbling about the strange cloudy skies, but other than that, things seemed to be settling down a bit. Mike the cook had placed a large empty pickle jar on the counter at the diner, and on it said 'The Eli and Pinky Fund'. He was not surprised to see it filling up fast. Even some truckers who had stopped by for a quick meal were stuffing the jar with money. Mike the cook always thanked everyone, then would happily tell the whole story to anyone who would listen.

Pinky, Jeanne and little Charlotte arrived home just about 11 AM. Jeanne saw how tired Pinky looked and ordered her to take a nap. The baby had already been fed and changed. Pinky put her down in the bassinette she had bought, but rolled it into her bedroom. She laid down and fell asleep as soon as her head hit the pillow.

Mazer called, asking all kinds of questions. She told Jeanne she was going to come by early that evening. She said Alex was so excited to see his new little niece.

THE TRUCK STOP

When Eli got to the truck stop he headed to the restrooms first. After that he wanted to eat, then scan the place to find anyone heading toward Alton. He sat in a booth, while he gobbled down two burgers, some fries and a shake. He tried the pay phones and called several numbers. They were either busy or there was no answer. He was scanning the busy dining area, and then he spotted the man. The guy was huge, taller than Eli and seemed to be ordering enough food for three people. His beard was down to his chest and he had a denim shirt on with the sleeves cut off. He had a hat on his head that said 'Patriots- Superbowl Champions', but when Eli saw one of his tattoos on his left bicep, he knew this was the right guy. The tattoo was a beautiful colored eagle that carried a banner that said Semper Fi. An ex-Marine he thought and his spirits lifted as he walked over to the giant of a man and tapped him on the shoulder. When the guy turned around he smiled at Eli and said, "Semper Fi Soldier." Eli smiled back and started telling his story and how important it was for Eli to get home as fast as possible. The man grabbed his food, looked down at Eli and said, "No problem. I got nothing but time until morning. Let's hit the road now." Eli actually jumped and ran to his booth, cleared off his stuff and grabbed his duffel bag. He followed right behind this big man, who had to be at least 6 FT.7 inches tall and about 300 Lbs. of pure muscle. As he sat in the cab of the truck, he closed his eyes and thought, hang on Pinky, I'll be home soon. Off they drove, and as Lion (his real name was Lionel, but no one even dared to call him that) ate his four burgers while he hummed an old Willy Nelson song, On the Road Again. It was well past dawn now, and far off in the distance, the sky seemed gray with very strange clouds. Lion hadn't told him that he had to make a couple of stops along the way. The first stop was at a small trailer park where his mother lived. He had a package for her and also told Eli his Uncle Percy was visiting, so he might be about a half hour. Eli told him that he would wait in the truck, but the half hour turned into almost two hours when the cab door finally opened and Lion sat himself down. "Sorry about that." he said as he started the truck and rode off again. His next stop was at a small motorcycle shop an hour later. He told Eli that he had to check on his Harley Davidson that was being repaired. Eli was getting agitated again as another hour went by. He also noticed that it was actually starting to drizzle. Almost a little after 3 PM. they were on the road again. Alton was about two hours away, and Eli was becoming very anxious. His only thoughts were about Pinky. Lion pulled the truck over at the exit sign that was bent and battered, but still could be read. It said Alton with an arrow pointing the correct way to the town. Eli tossed his bag out, jumped from the cab and thanked Lion over and over. "No problem" Lion said, "My pleasure, glad I could help a fellow Marine, little man." Eli started walking, feeling drops of rain coming down harder. He walked down the exit as fast as he could, heading toward the Main Street of his town.

Part Seven

Smiling Mazer
The Return Of Jacob
The beginning of the End

SMILING MAZER

Many of the towns people had been stopping by Pinky's during the day. They all brought gifts and food, only staying long enough to see the new baby and ask for any of the latest news about Eli.

Mazer was too excited to sit around the house. She made a quick lunch for her and Alex, just put the dishes in the sink, then looked at Alex and said, "Let's go to Pinky's early to see the new baby now." Alex didn't have to be told twice, so as Mazer changed, he went to wash up and find a clean shirt to put on. He had been in his room looking at the shiny padlock which he had hidden under all his socks in the old bureau in his bedroom. He put it away quickly, found a clean shirt, brushed his teeth and combed his hair. He could hear Aunt Mazer jiggling the keys to the Studebaker. He ran out of his room to grab the keys, but then looked at Cooper. Aunt Mazer had told him he would have to stay at the farm, but between Alex and the dog, he finally convinced her that Cooper would be a good boy and that he should also be able to see the new baby. "After all," Alex said, "Cooper is part of the family too." Aunt Mazer looked at the dog and saw he had on his please take me with you look and easily gave in to both of them. Alex and Cooper ran out to the garage , started up the car, slid over as Aunt Mazer got in and they were soon on their way. They arrived at Pinky's house and Alex helped carry in the packages they had brought. The baby was awake and soon was in the arms of Aunt Mazer. "She is perfect." she said. Alex looked at the baby and came to the conclusion that it was just a baby. He didn't know what all the fuss was about, even Cooper sniffed her a minute, looked at Alex and had the same look on his face. Alex then saw all the fancy food that had been arranged on the table. For him, that was more interesting so he headed over to the table and started eating, especially all the different desserts that were available. Cooper just sat next to him and sure enough, Alex snuck him a couple of treats. Everyone did notice though when Cooper walked over to the baby's bassinette and laid down next to her. The dog knew she was a special addition.

Pinky was showing all the wonderful gifts that had been given to her during the day. Mazer was so happy for Pinky and little Charlotte. She also kept commenting on how just about everything was pink. Jeanne had laughed about that also and said, "Did you even think otherwise?' Mazer could sense the feeling of happiness all around everyone, but also saw how tired Pinky looked. After a while she grabbed Alex, who was still stuffing his mouth with desserts at the table, and told him it was time to head back to the farm. She hugged Pinky so hard and Pinky understood why. Alex had just enough time to grab a third brownie before they left the house and walked to the car. On the ride home all Aunt Mazer did was rave about how beautiful the baby was and was smiling from ear to ear. All of a sudden Alex shouted, "Hey, Aunt Mazer, it's starting to rain a little." Sure enough, a light drizzle had changed to rain drops, and Mazer said, "Thank God, it's about time."

THE RETURN OF JACOB

It was later in the afternoon and the house was quiet. Everyone had left, and the table was cleared and wiped down. Jeanne smiled to herself as she thought at least Pinky would not have to do any cooking for Eli for quite a while. Jeanne let out a sigh as she sat in the recliner and put her feet up. She had actually ordered Pinky to take another nap and this time Pinky didn't even try to argue with her. She felt so tired and nervous and had been constantly looking out the front window for any signs of Eli.

In the silence of the house Jeanne could hear the baby gurgling and cooing in her bassinette. "Oh that little angel," she thought. She could hardly wait for Eli to walk through the door. The new family in town would then be complete. She heard the rain on the windows and knew the farmers would be so relieved. She picked up the new book she had started two days ago and began reading. It was one of those romance novels she liked so much and this one was proving to be especially spicy. With the book in her lap and the sound of the rain she felt she could almost doze off. She heard thunder in the distance, and noticed that Charlie the cockatiel was becoming agitated for some reason, flitting from one side of his cage to the other. Jeanne swore he was saying "Eli's coming, Eli's coming." She looked at the bird and told him to be quiet, she didn't want him to wake Pinky up. She started to look for the large pink square of cloth that Pinky used to cover the bird's cage at night. She stopped as she realized she heard footsteps in the kitchen. The rain was coming down in torrents now, even pounding on the roof. Her heart was racing for a reason, and when she turned to look towards the kitchen doorway, she saw him. A dark figure with muddy boots in a black rain parka. As he pulled the hood of the parka down, she gasped, took a step back and said, "It's you!" She wanted to scream and warn Pinky, but as she finally found the strength to do so, there was a blow to the side of her head and she fell unconscious on the brick floor in front of the fireplace.

Jacob was like a madman. He took his large hunting knife (the one he had stolen from Benny's hardware store) and began slashing the cushions on the couch and recliner. He threw a small pillow at the birdcage and knocked it over, feathers flying everywhere. He started throwing pictures and Knick Knacks into the fireplace, while angrily muttering to himself. He held a picture of Bill Jr. and Virginia Rosker and the boys, then spit on it and threw it across the room. He grabbed the telephone near the couch, cut the wires off then just threw it on the floor. He looked at himself in the small antique mirror which hung on one of the walls, then smashed it with the hilt of his knife. He was breathing hard. He was so filled with anger and hate. How dare this town and its people still have so much, especially since his brother had banned him from it so many years ago. The town was supposed to have withered and died. Instead, people still helped each other. Businesses had still held on and the people had actually acted like one big family. He was sputtering and shaking, and the anger he felt was overwhelming him when he suddenly saw he was face to face with Jenn Pinkton , and she was holding a pink bundle in her arms as hard as she could. He took two steps closer to her and stared. She was a beauty. He also saw the baby in her arms. It seemed as though a dark light went on in his head and he smiled. Pinky could see he had few teeth, and cringed as he spoke, seeing spittle not only dripping down his chin but flying everywhere. His thoughts were evil and Pinky could sense it. He looked at her and said, "Yes, that's it. With the loss of you and that baby, the town would finally die, it would finally have to mourn and be forgotten, like I was supposed to be, as my brother had made me do. To forget his own brother and deny him of his rightful place in this town." The rain was falling so hard that Pinky doubted anyone would hear her scream for help. Jacob suddenly grabbed the baby away from Pinky. She panicked now, begging for her little one. He laughed like a madman again. Even though he was slipping on the blood next to Jeanne's head, he bent down , grabbed one of Jeanne's ankles and dragged her body into the small kitchen. He pushed Pinky down hard onto the recliner, as she was begging and crying for her little daughter. He kept looking around and then cut a long piece of fabric from the couch. He ordered her to stand up and turn around, then placed the pink bundle of baby on the couch. When he told her to put her hands behind her back she shook her head, then he hit her hard in the back. He shouted at her again, then with an evil grimace told her next time he would hit the baby. Pinky was crying and pleading with him, but then did put her hands behind her. He tied her wrists together tightly and pushed her down onto the recliner again. He was just glowering at her, and she could feel his evil thoughts. He seemed to be mumbling to himself, and thought about the old truck, the one he had stolen from the Choates farm. He was glad he had parked it in the small area behind the house. His plan would be simpler now. He grabbed Pinky's arm and stood her up. He also picked up the baby and held her with one arm close to him. In his other hand was the large hunting knife. He pushed her towards the kitchen and told her to head for the door and get in the truck. She was crying hysterically when she saw Jeanne on the floor and was also trying to look at Charlotte. He smacked her in the face and just pushed her out the door, but not before he reached into his pocket and threw a small piece of paper on the floor next to Jeanne that said 'This town is going to die' He made her climb into the truck and as she slid over to the other side of the seat, he slammed the door shut. He put the baby between them on the front seat, but kept the large knife in his right hand while he backed up the truck. He knew exactly where he needed to go. Pinky kept glancing at Charlotte all bundled up in the thick, pink blanket. The baby was awake, her eyes wide open and she was still making gurgling sounds now and then. Pinky was also thinking about Jeanne. Poor Jeanne, on the kitchen floor, and she started to cry again.

The rain was coming down heavier now and the wind had started to almost howl. Every few minutes a large streak of lightening could be seen , followed by extremely loud episodes of thunder. The earth had been so dry, too dry and was not even absorbing the heavy rain. Large puddles were forming everywhere. No one was out on the streets. The lights from the houses on Main Street were flickering on and off at times. Storm warnings and weather updates kept flashing on televisions all over town, and people just huddled in their homes and watched the storm seem to grow in strength.

Eli was walking as fast as he could. His left ankle, the one that had been badly sprained while he was in Afghanistan, was really hurting. He winced every time he put pressure on it, feeling the pain shooting up to the calf of his leg. This did not stop him, or slow down Eli's mission to get to Pinky's house. Ten more minutes he told himself. Main St. was empty, with only the sounds of thunder, the gale winds and the rain falling. It was coming down so hard Eli was soaked through and through. He passed the small theatre that had been closed for four years. The hardware store was dark, along with Carl's Butcher Shop. Then he saw the small pink house and sprinted awkwardly through the gate of the picket fence. Lightening streaked across the sky and the sound of thunder soon followed again. He opened the front door and immediately knew something was terribly wrong. The couch was all torn apart, glass and shards of ceramic bits littered the floor. The birds cage was laying on the floor near the front window, but he saw Charlie flying from window to window shouting, "Eli's back, Eli's back." Then he saw the blood, and a trail of it leading into the kitchen. He called out for Pinky several times as he checked the bedroom, but saw no one. The telephone and wires on the side of one of the end tables had been cut and were thrown on the floor. He dropped his duffle bag and noticed all the damage. Charlie had flown onto the mantle of the fireplace, which was bare except for a few broken pieces of the Knick Knacks that Pinky displayed there.

All of a sudden he heard a sound. He stood silent and reached for Charlie to quiet the bird, who walked up Eli's arm and just sat on his shoulder. He heard the sound again, like a moan and ran to the kitchen. There, on the floor he saw Jeanne, with blood all around here head. She was trying to sit up and open her eyes, but kept holding her head. Eli felt Charlie fly from his shoulder and he leaned over and propped Jeanne up against the kitchen wall. "Jeanne, Jeanne, what happened ? Where's Pinky, what the hell happened here?" Jeanne was starting to cry and found it hard to talk. She took a deep breath and slowly opened her eyes. "Eli, oh Eli." She was astounded to see him standing over her. "Oh my God, you have to save them, you have to save them, Pinky and the baby." She felt faint again and Eli just shook her a little. "Stay with me Jeanne, who took Pinky and what baby?" Jeanne blinked her eyes and squinted. "Eli, Pinky had the baby, a little girl." Eli had a look of shock on his face then asked Jeanne again, " Who took them, what happened?" Jeanne then seemed to be more coherent and told him everything that had happened. She was crying again as she looked at him and said ,"It was Jacob, can you believe that, it was Jacob all along."

Eli was beside himself. He saw a piece of paper on the floor. He picked it up and read "This towns going to die." He dropped the paper and looked at Jeanne again. "Where did he take her, where, did he say anything? Do you remember anything?" Jeanne took a deep breath and Eli thought she was on the verge of passing out again. He shook her again and she responded right away. "I'm awake, I'm awake, let me think a minute." She was staring off toward the backdoor, which was open. Jeanne started telling Eli how Jacob was angrily rambling on about the town and that it was his also, all of it. She also remembered being dragged into the kitchen, and she heard the sound of a truck in the back. Eli had grabbed a pack of frozen vegetables from the freezer, and told Jeanne to hold it on the massive lump that had formed on her head. That seemed to help, but Jeanne's memory was still foggy. "Wait, wait" she said. Just before she passed out again, she thought she heard him mumbling about the forest and the trees. She shook her head and the throbbing increased. "Help me up, Eli, please. I have to stand up for a minute. Get me one of the kitchen chairs, I'll sit." The iced package was helping. Her vision was clearer, as was her speech. He helped her sit in one of the chairs, then like a light going on in his brain he said, "I know where he is taking her."

He saw the keys to Pinky's small VW Beetle hanging on the wall, he grabbed them and started out the door. Jeanne was shouting at him "Where are you going Eli, where?" He dragged her on the chair over to the phone that was hanging on the wall near the sink. He was running as best he could out the back door when he told Jeanne "Call Mazer right away! Tell her everything."

He ran around to the side driveway where Pinky's old VW Beetle was parked. It was a crème color and of course had pink flowers on it. As he got in the car, he remembered telling Pinky he would never be caught dead driving that thing He revved the engine and backed out of the driveway, saying to himself, I'm coming Pinky, just hang on. I'm on my way. The car was not meant to be used in this weather. It kept swerving and sliding and was not moving any faster than 60 miles per hour. Before long though he was out of town and heading to one of the main logging roads. The rain was coming down so hard, even the wipers on the car couldn't keep up. Small trees had fallen, but he was lucky as he avoided hitting any of them. He was pushing the little car as much as he could, and he felt he was almost there. It had been years since he traveled any of the old logging roads and prayed he was going the right way. The small headlights on the little car were not that bright, so he was thankful every time a streak of lightening lit up the forest. He felt he was heading a bit downhill now, and that was where he needed to go, to the 'Tree of Stories' that sat at the edge of the ravine above the river.

The small car was starting to sputter and slow down. No, no, not now he said to himself. The car did come to a slow stop on the side of one of the logging roads. Eli looked at the gas gauge, it was on empty.

He pounded the steering wheel, cursing and yelling at the car. He had no idea how far he was from the Tree of Stories. The forest was so dark, between the clouds and sheets of rain falling down, he could hardly see. He had left his duffle bag at Pinky's house and thought how stupid that was. He could of changed into dryer clothes, plus he always carried a small flashlight in the bag. He knew now the only thing he could do was walk, so he trudged onward

Mazer was balancing a folded load of laundry when she picked up the phone. She heard Jeanne's frantic voice and the laundry fell to the floor. "Calm down Jeanne, calm down," she continued to say as she listened to thc story. Alex was standing in the doorway of his bedroom, all ears while he pet Cooper. "Jeanne, are you sure, your positive it was Jacob?" Mazer could feel the anger rising in her. She knew it, the lights at the Great house, all the break- ins and the murders. Jacob she thought. That man had an evil air about him that she had sensed even on the first day she had met him. She hung up the phone. Jeanne said she was going to call the Sheriff's office, and also call Eileen, to keep her aware of what was happening. She knew that Gerry had not been feeling well at all that day, so Mike closed the diner early and they both headed home. Mazer had told Jeanne to go to the clinic right away.

Mazer was just standing there, feeling her anger take over and thinking. She was gritting her teeth when her decision was made. As she was putting on her boots and looking through the closet for her rain parka, she yelled out to Alex that she had to go out for a while, and for him to stay at the house. Little did she know that Alex had heard everything, and was determined to go along with her no matter what. He had quietly opened his bedroom window, put on a rain jacket and climbed out, with Cooper right behind him. He knew that if he had made Cooper stay in the room he would start barking loudly, which would have alerted Aunt Mazer. He hadn't realized how hard the rain was falling. His sneakers were already soaked when he walked through the side door of the garage. He slowly opened the back door of the Studebaker, and laid down on the floor, holding Cooper down by his side.

A minute later he heard the front garage door slide open. Mazer got in the driver seat, started the car up and backed out. She didn't stop to close the garage door, just sped off in the direction of the forest, and cursing most of way. Alex looked at Cooper, who was laying as still as can be and thought to himself that he had never remembered Aunt Mazer driving so fast, which told him something really bad must of happened.

Eileen had gotten the call from Jeanne, who was headed to the clinic. Jeanne was upset because she only connected to the answering machine at the Sheriff's office. She told the whole incident to Eileen, then told her she would call again later with more news. Eileen had just closed the convenience store and shouted to Dave to close up the garage also. With this storm, she sincerely doubted anyone would be venturing out. She sat at her desk, staring at the phone, almost willing it to ring. She couldn't just sit there anymore, she grabbed her raingear and hollered to Dave. He came in wiping the rain from his hair and face. "What's up Ma?" "Just get in the Rover, I'll tell you all about it on the way. We have to go to Carl's house." He just stood there until she shouted at him, "Let's go, let's go." He grabbed the extra rain parka hanging from the peg near the door and out they went. They had never seen it rain this hard before, and thunder still boomed every time the lightening lit up the town. The wind had picked up and was blowing all kinds of debris in the air and all over Main St. The Land Rover was meant for this weather as Eileen drove as fast as she could toward Carl's house. Sure enough, she saw the Sheriff's cruiser parked in front and also noticed Willy Grey Wolf's pickup. The lights were still flickering on and off again in the town. Dave loudly knocked at the front door and then just walked in. Eileen and her son looked like two drowned rats as they wiped their feet and slid their parka's off. The Sheriff stood up, as did Willy Grey Wolf.. "Oh no, now what?" said the Sheriff. Then Eileen began telling her the whole story.

THE BEGINNING OF THE END

Eli knew he was heading the right way because he could feel the slope of the forest increasing as he half sprinted, half limped along the logging trail he was on. The rain was falling so hard and fast that rivulets had formed and were pushing branches, clumps of leaves and even small stones down the slope. He had even seen a few small saplings uproot and travel the course of the trails. He had tripped on a root base and fallen a while back, but managed to free his foot and again walk as fast as he could. Then he saw it. A small clearing was up ahead and he could even hear the gushing water of the river. He had to be close. Another large streak of lightening lit up the forest. He then saw a figure on the ground in front of the huge tree. Another figure was standing a few feet away, almost too close to the edge of the ravine. Eli had a plan. He crawled on his stomach to the standing figure, but just as he rose to tackle Jacob, another bolt of lightning lit up the entire area. He still jumped but did not see the shining blade of the large hunter's knife, although he did feel it pierce his left shoulder. He fell down and rolled, feeling blood oozing from the wound, but was also looking straight into Pinky's eyes when he stopped rolling. Pinky screamed and he pushed his body towards hers. Pinky was still screaming, then Eli looked at the man that was standing over him. The man who was holding a pink bundle under his arm. Eli laid next to Pinky, and saw blood trickling down from under his sleeve. He tried to ignore the pain, but saw Pinky tied to the tree and crying uncontrollably. He touched her leg and tried to calm her down. He told her he loved her so much, but felt useless as he stared at Jacob.

Jacob had backed away from both of them, and started laughing. He then said, "This is perfect, what more could I ask for." He continued to stare at both of them, then kicked Eli as hard as he could. Eli would not show any pain, he wouldn't give Jacob that satisfaction. Jacob had kicked Eli on his left side, and now Eli knew his ribs were cracked again. He could see Pinky in a state of shock, just staring at the baby and crying. Jacob backed away a few steps, screaming and laughing at the same time. All Eli could think of was this man was totally insane, and he meant to kill them all.

The logging trails weren't that wide and the torrents of rain were pushing all kinds of large branches, mounds of pine cones and any other debris in its way. The Studebaker was driving through it all though, and Mazer held onto the wheel even as it became airborne when it hit a small deadfall. It was so dark in the forest that Mazer reached for the switch for the third light and found that the extra bit of illumination did help. "Please God" she said, "Let me make it in time." She then heard a soft whine from the back seat. She was a bit confused, but hung on to the steering wheel while looking in the back seat area. "Alex "she screamed., "What are you doing there?" Alex slowly got up from the floor and sat down on the back seat with Cooper right next to him. Mazer was frantic and screaming at him. All he said was "I just wanted to help, honest." She looked at him from the rearview mirror, and managed to control her anger. "Alex, you listen to me, you hear me, I said listen. I'm going to slow the car down and when I do you're going to open that backdoor and jump out as fast as you can. Do you understand, do you hear me?" Cooper was whining and Alex was crying. Again Mazer shouted to him

"You do as I say. Do you hear me? Say you understand now!" Alex nodded and said yes as he slid over to left side of the passenger door. Another flash of lightning, and all of a sudden Mazer saw Jacob holding the baby out toward the ravine. She also saw Pinky and Eli on the ground right against the huge Maple, the Tree of Stories. She couldn't think fast enough, but took a deep breath and slowed the car down just enough to see Alex open the door and roll out on the forest floor. Cooper followed right behind him. She instantly sped up again heading toward the Tree of Stories. She didn't know how fast she was driving, but the next strike of lightening, which seemed to be brighter than most of the other strikes, gave her the extra light she needed.

Alex had stood up and started running, following the taillights of the Studebaker. Cooper had other plans, and passed him running a pace like a race horse.

The anger in Mazer's face was immeasurable, as Jacob turned and looked confused when he saw an object with three lights heading right for him. The confusion increased as he felt something jump at him and grab the pink bundle from under his arm. Mazer did not think twice as the Studebaker hit him broadside and he tumbled over the ravine into the raging river below, followed by the car and Mazer as she still held the steering wheel with all her might.

Cooper landed solidly on all fours, and carefully carried the pink bundled baby girl over to Eli and laid her gently in his lap. He then turned and ran as he saw Alex starting toward the ravine.

Alex knew what had happened, since he saw the tail lights fading from view. He fell to his knees and started screaming, "No, No, Aunt Mazer, come back." He was sobbing and pounding the earth. "Why, Why, my Aunt Mazer, I just want you to come back." He kept crying then heard Eli call his name. "Alex, we need your help. Alex, do you hear me?" Alex looked toward the tree and saw Pinky tied and Eli was trying to get up, but kept falling back against the tree. Alex always kept his Boy

Scout jack knife in his pocket. He took it out and ran over to Pinky. He cut the rope from the tree and also cut the cord around her wrists. Alex caught her as she then leaned on Eli a bit and then Eli started calling her name. She finally opened her eyes and could hear the baby crying.

A few minutes later they heard the sound of other vehicles. They saw the headlights coming toward them and then skid to a stop. Eileen had been driving with Dave in the first vehicle, the Land Rover. The Sheriff had come with Carl and Willy Grey Wolf in the cruiser, which had been sliding around the entire way. They all ran to Eli and Pinky. Alex was sitting near the edge of the ravine and just stared. He heard Eli telling all of them what had happened, then felt Uncle Willy's arm around his shoulder. Alex started sobbing again and turned, burying his face into Uncle Willy's jacket. "Why?" he asked. "Why would she leave me, tell me why?" Willy Grey Wolf looked over the edge of the ravine. The river was moving so fast, even tearing up small trees as it churned its way with such a force. He looked up the river, but could not see any evidence of the Studebaker. He knew the river went on for miles, but was hoping the car would be caught on either some large stones or old stumps along the way. He had no answers for Alex, and just held him tightly while the boy continued to sob. He saw Cooper walking their way, and noticed he was badly limping. The dog just sat down and stared at Alex.

Eileen had a first aid kit in the Rover. She cut off one sleeve of Eli's shirt and saw all the blood. She yelled to Willy, "We have to get them to the clinic as fast as possible." Pinky would not let go of the baby, so Carl came over and picked her and the baby right up and put her in the Land Rover. Dave helped Eli into the Rover also. Sheriff Lambert and Carl would follow in the cruiser. Willy, Dave and Eileen would go on ahead since the Rover was more suited to the forest terrain. Alex sat in the back of the cruiser, but not before Willy picked Cooper up and laid him next to Alex.

About 20 minutes later, they arrived at the clinic. Doc Horton and the staff were stunned when they all came through the doors. The Dr. and his staff went into immediate action. Eli needed sutures right away, and Pinky was examined by one of the nurses. She still would not let go of the baby, who was soaked and shivering. Pinky started yelling, "No, no, no one is taking my baby." The nurse knew she was in shock and began pleading with her. All of a sudden Jeanne appeared. She had been resting in another area, waiting for the results of her x-rays. She told the nurse to step aside, then started talking soothingly to Pinky. "Sweetie" she said. "We have to change little Charlotte. We don't want her to get sick, right?" Pinky nodded and held out the baby to Jeanne, who instantly went into "nurse mode" again. After dry clothes, a fresh diaper and a thorough exam, Jeanne walked around with the baby in her arms , but did not leave Pinky's sight. Pinky seemed to be coming around and stayed calm as long as she could see little Charlotte. Carl ,Gerry and Mike had been with Jeanne. Sheriff Lambert choked up when Gerry asked where Mazer was. There was silence. Willy Grey Wolf came over and started to talk in a quiet voice, and told them what had happened. Gerry let out a cry and Mike put his arms around her.

Three hours later the clinic was quiet again. The Dr. had given Eli something for the pain and he was now resting comfortably. Pinky had changed into a dry Johnny, and was sipping at a cup of tea, The baby was sleeping peacefully. Jeanne had rummaged through a box of donated clothes and had found a little outfit and blanket for the baby, and guess what, they were pink. One of the plastic bassinettes had been brought in and the baby stayed right next to Pinky. Jeanne's x-rays had been viewed by Doc Horton, and all was well. She would just have a lump for a few days. "You have a hard head" said the Dr. Jeanne laughed and told him that's what her husband had always told her. Willy Grey Wolf cornered the Dr. and told him that Cooper was limping quite a bit. "Well, I'm not a vet but let me look at it." Sure enough, he found one large cut on the pad of his right foot. He cleansed it, put antibiotic ointment on it and wound a bandage around the paw. He told Willy the dog would be fine, then also said, "That dog's quite a hero, I've been told." Now Willy Grey Wolf had tears in his eyes and replied "Him and Mazer, they saved them all."

Alex would not talk. He just sat in a chair in the hall and stared into space. Gerry and Carl were sitting on either side of him. Carl just kept shaking his head while Gerry tried not to cry. They were all worried about Alex, but didn't know what to say. Sister Madeline and Sister Teresa had ridden down to the clinic. They both said the rain had stopped, even though thunder could still be heard in the distance. Pinky was up and feeling much better. Jeanne had found a robe for her, but jokingly apologized because it was blue. The nuns came in to look at little Charlotte and raved about her bright green eyes. Eli stirred in the bed and asked for some water. Sister Teresa was out the door of his room and back so fast as she held the cup for him as he drank. He then saw Pinky by his bed, holding the little one. She cradled the baby next to him and said, "I'd like to officially introduce you to your little daughter, Charlotte Pearl." He kept saying over and over how tiny she was and kissed her on the head. Pinky leaned over and they kissed, feeling their love bond them forever.

Sister Madeline had always had a special gift with children. She walked over to Alex, kneeled in front of him and took his hands in hers. Carl and Gerry left them alone for a while. Sister Madeline looked straight at Alex and said, "I know how much pain you are feeling, I really do. But I also know that your Aunt Mazer is so proud of you. She had great faith and raised you to be strong. She loves you so much, and you should always remember that." He put his arm around her and said, "She was brave also," and started telling the nun the whole story. She knew he would be fine and said a prayer of thanks.

A nurse from the next shift came running into the clinic, almost breathless, "You've got to see this, you won't believe it. Everyone's coming out of their houses to see it. Come out , everyone."

Jeanne, Gerry, Mike and Carl followed by Sheriff Lambert and Doc Horton walked out the doors and into the street. "It looks like snow" Mike said, "but that's impossible." Then Gerry said, "They're feathers, tiny white feathers." They were falling everywhere, sticking to the wet cars, sidewalks and houses. Eileen and Dave had been standing near the Land Rover and just kept looking up. The small white wisps of feathers were covering all of them, gracefully falling from the sky. The stars were out now and even the moon could be seen. It was almost full. "Holy Mackerel" Dave said, " Where are they coming from?" Sister Madeline was next to him. She raised her face to the sky and felt the feathers covering her. She then said, "It's a sign from above, there's a special Angel looking over all of us," and just smiled as she enjoyed seeing the white feathers fall all over the town.

EPILOGUE

Martin looked up at the sky and smiled. The sun was out and a warm breeze was blowing. His farm was quite a ways from the town of Alton, but he had heard all the stories. He was taking advantage of the good weather to clean up any debris around the house and barn. It was still very wet in areas, even some large puddles had prompted him to wear his mud boots. Gullies on the sides of the road continued flowing full force toward the drains that ended before his property. He heard his wife, Sonja, tell him lunch was ready. As he hung his small shovel on its hook, he looked up the road. He was surprised to see a dark figure limping up that way of the road. His small barn pickup was close and had the keys in it. He thought of taking a quick ride up there to see if the person needed any help. His wife Sonja called again, "Martin your lunch is getting cold, get in here now. I mean it." He kept watching the figure as he took off his boots and went in the house to eat. The figure in the dark coat was limping. It also noticed the gushing of water on each side of the road. All of a sudden the person reached down and grasped something being washed away by the rivulets that had formed. It was a gray striped scrawny kitten about 5 weeks old. It was soaking wet, but still managed to let out a healthy meow. The kitten looked at the stranger with eyes wide open. One eye was green, the other was yellow. Hmm, said the person, for some reason I'm supposed to know you, but I can't remember why. The kitten was then nestled into the inside pocket of the coat, staying warm and dry, as the figure continued walking on.

THE END?

CPSIA information can be obtained
at www.ICGtesting.com
Printed in the USA
JSHW022052010722
27611JS00001BA/7